Black

& other plays

Black Beach
& other plays

Edited by
Jeff Teare & Jordi Coca

Parthian
The Old Surgery
Napier Street
Cardigan
SA43 1ED

www.parthianbooks.co.uk

ISBN 978-1-905762-81-1

Cover design by Lucy Llewellyn
Inner design & typsetting by books@lloydrobson.com
Printed and bound by Dinefwr Press, Llandybïe, Wales

CYNGOR LLYFRAU CYMRU
WELSH BOOKS COUNCIL

Published with the financial support of the Welsh
Books Council.

Contents

Introduction – Catalan Theatre Today

It is generally agreed that Catalan theatre is now exper-
iencing a minor renaissance and that probably circumstances
have never been so favourable for staging drama. In the
democratic transition after the dictatorship from 1976,
Catalonia recovered part of its sovereignty via a Statute of
Autonomy that at least guaranteed complete control over
some areas, such as culture. Politicians in the new situation
were also very sensitive to the fact that theatre is not
possible without audiences and that consequently it is a
pre-eminently social art. In any case, it is hardly surprising
that the greatest historical periods for the stage have
coincided with democratic forms of government, whatever
the idiosyncrasies of the particular political models.

The fact is that from 1980 public money began to be
set aside for Catalan theatre – the precedent was set in
municipal Barcelona in 1976 when the renowned, legendary
Grec-76 summer festival was organised – and the foundations
were thus laid for the current situation. However it would
be naïve to think a series of policies could spring generously
from nowhere. Previously, at least from 1946, there had
been a constant, difficult struggle to regain the right to
stage plays in Catalan, that had been banned, like so many
other things, by the Francoist dictatorship after 1939. A
group was created in 1954 that went by the name of
Agrupació Dramàtica de Barcelona (ADB), somewhat similar
to the Abbey Theatre founded in Ireland, led by the director
and critic Frederic Roda. The ADB, which was hugely
important aesthetically and ideologically, was banned in
1963. But, another project was established in 1960, which
was made possible by Ricard Salvat in collaboration with
leading representatives of Catalan culture. This was the

Escola Catalana d'Art Dramàtic Adrià Gual (EADAG) that functioned uninterruptedly until 1975. Both these bodies, and the Institut del Teatre that from 1970 was under the leadership of Hermann Bonnín, would encourage professional attitudes by teaching many elements then known as Independent Theatre. Also, the policy of awarding prizes for theatrical texts, largely driven by Frederic Roda, led to a proliferation of initiatives throughout Catalonia. Some gained an international profile as was the case with Els Joglars, or Comediants, and later the Fura del Baus.

Overall, very different aesthetic approaches were at work, from experimental theatre to the repertoire of great international theatre, encompassing the reclaiming of Catalan writers from all periods: mime, puppets, musical theatre.... All this was done from the perspective of resistance, taxing the tolerance of the dictatorship that over the years was forced to act slightly more flexibly. Nonetheless, we are talking about semi-professional companies, one-off shows or almost single performances, with close to minimal technical provision.

As previously mentioned, once the dictatorship was out of the way, the first public grants were made available in 1976. This is also the year when the Teatre Lliure (Free Theatre) was founded, led by Fabià Puigserver, a key player who, following the model of the Piccolo Teatro in Milan, set about overcoming previous artistic and technical shortcomings. In effect, with the help of public funding, the Lliure improved acting methods and stage design and construction, and the programming, management, profile and reputation of the theatre, now that audiences were slowly beginning to improve.

From 1980 constant pressure through the media and demands put on the new democratic politicians forced the autonomous government and town halls to orchestrate a specific cultural policy in relation to theatre that is open to criticism but which made the present flourishing panorama possible with all its virtues and failings: the creation of a Drama Centre of Catalonia, the creation of the Mercat de les Flors as a theatrical space, the later creation of the National Theatre of Catalonia, the expansion of the Teatre Lliure as part of these public or semi-public initiatives, the re-opening of theatres across the territory, support for private theatre, the publication of extensive bibliographies on theatre in Catalan, international contacts etc....

These are the developments that help explain the present, lively situation. At this particular moment in time a new generation of dramatists and theatre directors found they were able to put their talents to good use in acceptable contexts. There is an awareness that Catalan is a minority language that faces lots of problems even in the Catalan environment because of the societal bilingualism favoured by the dictatorship, but now it is clear that the theatre must go after new audiences by adapting to majority tastes. Coinciding with the appearance of a commercial theatre that had previously been practically non-existent because of the lack of a market, this inclusive policy provoked a big increase in what was on offer and a relative equilibrium between supply and demand.

The price paid, a price that was quite unnecessary and unfair, was the consigning to oblivion of all the past history we have just sketched, except for the figure of Fabià Puigserver and the works written by Josep Mª Benet i Jornet, that became a reference point for the new men and women of Catalan theatre.

The rest disappeared into the shadows of the past, triggering such unjust situations as, for example, the one where the National Theatre of Catalonia has taken eight to ten years to première such distinguished twentieth-century dramatists as, say, Joan Oliver, Carles Soldevila, Joan Brossa and Salvador Espriu, and still has not performed such first-rate writers as Josep Palau i Fabre, Maria Aurèlia Capmany and Manuel de Pedrolo.

All those authors who gave life to the Independent Theatre have also disappeared from an artistic point of view: Josep Mª Muñoz Pujol, Alexandre Ballester, Jaume Melendres, Rodolf Sirera, Jordi Teixidor, and Manuel Molins (one of the most interesting authors still writing now) and others.

Such is the present state of play. Programming for public theatre is very conservative, very close to the interests of the commercial stage, and proceeds without any risk-taking from an aesthetic, dramatic or ideological point of view. We are therefore waiting for a new generation of English-style angry young men or women able to shake up today's complacent and optimistic bourgeois outlook.

Nevertheless it would be wrong not to acknowledge that the consolidation of audiences and adaptation of programming policy to more conservative, insipid sensi-bilities has led to an increase in ticket sales and an increase in the strictly economic level of theatre business. And we must also acknowledge that there has never been such a flourishing of writers and directors working in various kinds of theatre: commercial theatre, popular theatre, Pinteresque theatre.... There is a very long roll-call of writers and I am aware I can only mention a very small sample: Jordi Galcerán, Sergi Bebel, Carol López, Albert Espinosa, Jordi Casanovas, Enric Nolla, Albert Mestres, Victòria Szpunberg, Marc Rosic, Emiliano Pastor, Gemma Rodríguez, Gerard Vàzquez, Carles Mallol.... There are many more and there are also many young directors beginning to appear.

But we must now focus on the three dramatists featured in this volume. Firstly I should like to make it clear that this selection does not imply an attempt to establish a hier-archy or to give the impression that the names presented, mine included, are more important than any other. The selection criteria have been influenced by a number of factors. On the one hand, there was the restriction on the number of characters in the works selected, stipulated by the publishers; on the other, rather than selecting authors from all those territories where Catalan is spoken, those referred to as the Catalan Countries and which include Catalonia, Valencia, the Balearic Islands, northern or French Catalonia and the Alguer, we wanted to offer a taste of what is being created in Catalan by authors from the area of Barcelona. Writing for the Valencian stage is as Catalan as for the Barcelona stage, but given that only three works could be published, and that territorial criteria weren't feasible, we decided to concentrate on Barcelona. Obviously, the choice is subjective (all choices are), made on the basis of very personal assumptions, however I have nevertheless taken into account the following issues:

a) The coherence of the work written in the case of Lluïsa Cunillé, an oeuvre rooted in Pinter which over the years has developed its own dense and profound world, without making concessions to the box-office. It has nonetheless won the respect of critics, academic opinion and the audience that follows her. The action in the work we offer develops in a concrete, real space but this doesn't prevent it from being a text that clearly eschews realist theatre.

b) In terms of what Joan Casas does, I took into account the fact that his project is different spatially. In effect, the place where his characters find themselves is an abstract space subordinate to the interplay of ambiguities of time that form part of the project. Casas is a man of the theatre, a poet, a narrator and translator from several languages, including Greek.

Because of factors I mentioned earlier, his work has lately not had the visibility it deserves.

c) My case is different (and how difficult it is to speak of oneself!): although I have had links with the world of the theatre from 1971, until recently I had only written novels. My writing for the stage is very recent, I don't start from Pinter and am particularly interested in articulating projects for a political theatre that shouldn't at all be confused with ideological theatre. The dramatic space is the stage itself, and it is not hard to see that 'Black Beach' is driven by a wish to rework the myth of Antigone.

Catalan theatre today has the added interest that it is a territory to be discovered, a new territory that springs logically from an adaptation of the main trends in European drama. In the Sixties and the Seventies Catalan authors were mainly influenced by Brecht for the obvious reason of their opposition to the dictatorship. Now the majority are inspired by the likes of Beckett, Pinter, and Bernhard. But some look to models such as the comedies of Woody Allen, the fragile worlds of Chekhov, or the formulaic intrigues of Agatha Christie plays. For good or for evil, one finds all sorts on the contemporary Catalan stage, and that should be a spur to make you want to take a closer look.

Jordi Coca
Translated by Peter Bush

Dramaturgical Note

Reading Jordi's introduction to these three, short Catalan plays I am immediately struck by how similar the current Catalonian situation he describes would seem to be to the Welsh theatre circumstance I worked in a decade or so ago.

I took over Made In Wales Stage Company in 1995 after ten years of working almost exclusively on new writing at the Theatre Royal, Stratford East in London. I was immediately struck by the vibrancy of new Welsh playwriting in English (it should be 'playwrighting' but I've given up that argument), and I soon learnt that a comparable energy existed in the Welsh language.

I worked with writers such as Roger Williams, Sian Evans, Christine Watkins, Othniel Smith and Lewis Davies who were easily equal to most of the people I'd come across in London and there were actors like Lowri Mae, James Westerway (RIP), Dorien Thomas, Sharon Morgan... I could go on, who were as good as anyone I'd ever worked with anywhere (and I have been in this business for thirty-five years).

If Jordi is right (I've only been to Barcelona once) then Catalonia is fortunate to be going through a similar theatrical purple patch (I'm not sure if Wales still is).

Both Catalonia and Wales have, to an extent, defined their theatrical culture in terms of its opposition to their pervading hegemony – Spanish and English. As Jordi says, in the end it's about money actually getting through to the talent. The money, however, will always have strings attached. In both Catalonia and Wales two of these strings are coloured 'nation' and 'language' and this does affect the work, both positively and negatively. Made In Wales was set up to work in English; in the end it was killed off because it couldn't really also work in Welsh; and it would appear that the battle between Castile and Aragon still continues in modern Spain.

The three plays in this volume however, show little nationalistic or linguistic damage. 'The Sale' and 'Naked' could take place almost anywhere (so long as it was warm enough for 'Naked') and 'Black Beach' could easily be set at a British Labour Party Fringe meeting in the early Eighties.

Jordi also talks about the disregard, even denial, of the playwrights of the recent past in modern Catalonian theatre. I think the same could be said for Wales, but there are others more qualified to comment.

And then Jordi goes on to the three plays in this volume:

'The Sale' by Lluisa Cunille.

I would agree with Jordi that this play is 'rooted in Pinter'. The play seems to me to be about personal need and disconnection, very modern concerns in any-one's dramaturgy. The characters only meet and relate, insofar as they do, due to an economic transaction. They are essentially solitary beings, somewhat adrift in the modern world, wanting a hand to hold but with little hope of finding one. The play lacks high drama (unlike 'Naked'); the characters have to define them-selves in the mundane, the everyday situations that are their truth.

The translator tells me that in Act 1, when Marta says, 'Listen... listen' to Glòria, she drops from the formal manner of addressing others into the informal, suggesting that an intimacy has developed between them. It's difficult to deal with this in English and we have to remember that we are dealing with English versions of these plays, not the originals.

'Naked' by Joan Casas.

This play reminds me of something, I believe by a Cuban writer, I saw at the RSC in the late Sixties. It's not exactly a Priestlean time play but it does feel a bit mid- twentieth century to me, except perhaps for the nudity. In Priestley's 'Dangerous Corner' one chance remark leads to disaster; second time around it is ignored and all is well. In 'Naked' we get three versions of the same situation; the first ends with sex, the second death and the third with an accusation, a confession and, maybe, some kind of resolution. The three versions of the scene are independent (apart from a brief moment between two and three) but influence each other, obviously with the photograph but more subtly with moments that could go either way. The play is elliptical, dealing in relativity and parallelism. The space in which 'Naked' takes place is specifically described and consciously theatrical. (It would certainly be hard to produce this play without a stage trap). The attic is almost a character in the play, influencing how the other characters behave through what it allows, and does not allow, to be revealed about and to the human protagonists.

'Black Beach' by Jordi Coca.

Jordi may not 'start from Pinter' but I don't think he entirely escapes him either. However, the stronger resonance for me is with a Seventies/Eighties English political theatre style: Story, Hare, Edgar, Brenton etc. On first reading I was clearly reminded of inter-minable SWP/TIE meetings, and post-meeting pub sessions, that I once sat through in Leicester and Coventry.

However, Jordi's not interested in ill-informed dissections of the political correctness of the Third

International... as 'She' says, 'You know what I regret about all this? That you and I have got hurt.... In the end, only people should count....' The play makes it obvious that, in its reality, this is not the case. We never quite know what the exact ideology apparently shared by the protagonists is but it is certainly clear that they exist in a political world in which even their sexual relationship becomes a bargaining counter. Jordi refers to 'Antigone' – two (main) characters, one location, real time, the individual against the state.... I take his point.

So, these plays do reveal more than a touch of Pinter, a dash of Chekhov, a hint of Beckett as well as more than a hint of a few more modern writers such as Hare, Edgar, even Kane (I wouldn't really know about Bernhard). I didn't personally get a lot of Woody Allen or Agatha Christie but, as noted previously, I'm dealing with these plays in English, not in Catalan, and cultural references/influences could well be lost in translation....

Overall, from my UK perspective, I must have read, seen and directed a few hundred 'new' plays over the last thirty years in England and Wales (some were by Irish and Scottish writers) and 'The Sale' strikes me as being fairly similar (in a good way, of course) to a lot of this work. 'Naked', while having very Thirties/Fifties echoes, lurches into Nineties 'in yer face' land. 'Black Beach' has more than a touch of the Seventies/Eighties but might also seem to have something to say to us about the current demise of 'New' Labour?

See what you think.

Jeff Teare

Black Beach

Jordi Coca

First performed at Espai Brossa, Barcelona
September 1999

Cast:

She   –   Rosa Cadafalch
He   –   Joan Massotkleiner
Stagehand   –   Andrés Moreno

Creative Team:

Director   –   Lurdes Barba

Translated into English by Richard Thomson

SINGLE ACT

SHE is about forty years old. HE is about fifty-seven, fifty-eight.

The stage of a theatre or conference hall, where a political meeting is due to take place the following night. There is a half-assembled dais, a lectern, etc. SHE, at a folding table, sorts and staples papers. She gets on with it quietly. The STAGEHAND enters and puts down some bits of wood or boxes somewhere.

STAGEHAND: Hey!

SHE: (*Continuing her work*) All right?

STAGEHAND: Fine.... Listen, we're going for a coffee... we'll finish unloading the rest later... OK?

SHE: OK.

STAGEHAND: Bye.

STAGEHAND leaves and SHE lights a cigarette. SHE smokes and carries on working; doesn't realise that HE is watching her. After a while, when she sees him, she reacts in surprise, and harshly.

SHE: What are you doing here?

HE: I've been watching you for a while. I thought you'd noticed.

SHE: No... (*indicating the boxes*) I thought maybe you were one of the people setting all this up. I didn't see you.

HE: I heard you were still here, and...

SHE: Yes, I'm behind with things.

HE: (*Approaching her*) Do you want me to help?

SHE: (*Sharply*) No. It's not necessary.

HE: (*As if he hasn't heard*) What needs doing?

SHE: Nothing, I told you. As you can see, I'm stapling up the report...

HE: (*Stapling some sheets of paper*) Like this?

SHE: You're very good at it, yes...

Pause.

HE: Are you going to be long?

SHE: No... (*referring to the people unloading*) I'll leave when they finish unloading. But there's no need for you to wait.

HE: Don't even think about it, I've got plenty of time.... (*Pause. He tries to make conversation*) Theatres are strange, aren't they, when they're empty?

SHE: Maybe they are.

HE: It's... I don't know... like magic.... Imagine it tomorrow evening, with all the delegates, all the guys...

SHE: And the women...

HE: (*Ironically*) All the lady and gentlemen delegates...

SHE sits down. Long pause.

HE: Is there much left to be unloaded?

SHE: I think there're some tables, and the chairs. I don't think they'll be long, that's why I want to get all this ready.

HE: Of course, I said I'd help... (*He starts helping again.*)

SHE: There's no need. Just tell me what you came to say.

HE: I didn't come to say anything. I'd heard you were still here and...

SHE: You've already said that.

Pause.

HE: (*A little irritated*) I can see you're in a mood.

SHE: I don't know what you mean...

HE: It's not about anything, but seeing as we've been working together again the last few weeks, I thought it'd be worth our while talking a bit.

SHE: So what have you and I got to talk about then?

HE: I don't know, about us, how everything's gone...

SHE: Everything's gone badly, you know that.

HE: Look, things change...

SHE: There are those that do and those that don't, and I think it would be best if you understood that I'm not one for stories, and I've got other things to think about.

HE: Right, but at least I'd be grateful if you let me say that...

SHE: Not again, please. That's enough.

Pause.

HE: Is there someone else?

SHE: (*Laughs*) Don't be ridiculous. (*About the work*) You're screwing it up.

HE stops working and tries to stroke her arm. SHE rejects him.

HE: I can see you're still pissed off.

SHE: (*Harshly*) Where's all this going?

HE: It's just I don't like the relationship we have...

SHE: We haven't got a relationship.

HE: You know what I mean. (*He tries to touch her again.*)

SHE: (*Forcefully*) Don't touch me.

HE: You're too hard.

SHE: I'm not hard at all.

HE: Yes you are, you're too hard with everything.

SHE: You're wrong, but I'm not going to argue with you.... If I was hard, things wouldn't go the way they do for me.

HE: Things go the way you want them to go. You're too demanding. I've told you that loads of times.

SHE: I can see you still have a high opinion of me.

Pause.

HE: All right. I did it badly. I'm sorry. I should have been clearer with you. I didn't know enough about it. You know what I'm like – I'm never sure, but me being wrong once doesn't...

SHE: You make me feel ridiculous. And really, I don't understand you. You let me get my hopes up, and you use me when it suits you, then you refuse to talk about the relationship, you give me a kicking and you disappear. And now you turn up for God knows what.

HE: I already said I was wrong. But you always want things to go at your own pace. Maybe you were going too fast, you were pushing me. You didn't give me time.

SHE: Don't get cynical.

HE: I'm not getting cynical in the slightest.

SHE: Well that's what it seems like.... We went for years seeing each other only when you felt like it...

HE: When I could, which is different...

SHE: What's the point of all of this? It's done, it's finished. We were together, you weren't interested in what I was proposing, you broke it off without a word. OK, fine, get out.

HE: I think you're oversimplifying.

SHE: Well, perhaps I am. Apparently, these days I tend to oversimplify things...

HE: Don't muddle the issue.

SHE: Oh, so I'm the one muddling the issue, am I? Look, I don't know what you're doing here. I don't know what you want, but I have no desire whatsoever to talk to you...

HE: (*Approaching her*) I've already told you what I want. I found out you were here. I just want us to be friends.

SHE: What's wrong with you? Are you that desperate for a fuck? You blokes are a load of shites.

HE: That's not it.

SHE: Please, just leave me alone.

HE: Look, I didn't come to see you to have an argument, I swear that's not why I came.

SHE: I'm tired. I don't want an argument either. I can't, I haven't got it in me.... Go away, please. I'd rather be alone.

HE: That's a bit much. You're treating me as if I don't have any feelings...

SHE: Let's not get into feelings. I remember talking about all that a few times before.

HE: Perhaps then neither of us was really able to see it as it should have been.

SHE: Maybe.... The whole thing... it's too complicated. And ridiculous. (*She sits on a folding chair.*)

Pause.

HE: Is it so difficult, what I'm asking for?

SHE: (*Tired*) I don't know what you're asking for.... (*She goes through her pockets looking for cigarettes.*) Have you got any cigarettes?

HE: Yes. (*He gives her a cigarette and a light, then squats down.*) We don't get much chance to talk in peace.

SHE: The people with the platforms'll be coming.

HE: Doesn't matter.

SHE gets up and walks slowly, smoking. Pause.

SHE: What are your children up to?

HE: They're fine. Getting on with life, you know.

SHE: You're right.... We're like idiots.

They look at each other. HE approaches and touches her lips, and kisses her gently. SHE gives way and they hug.

HE: (*Embracing her*) I wish we could make our peace.

SHE: (*Taking a deep breath*) If only it was as simple as that.

HE: (*Half joking*) It can't be absolutely impossible.

Pause.

SHE: You don't understand.

HE: What don't I understand?

SHE: (*Sincerely*) I don't know how to explain.... It's things that, when you say them, they sound ridiculous, but I feel them right here, in my chest.... One day I started to feel we'd been saying the same thing for too long, doing the same things. I realised my mother was an old woman. You know what I mean? No, she wasn't an elderly lady, she was old, an old woman. And it wasn't just my mother. Everything around me was old, horribly old, and sad. The party was as well.... I thought about the times we spent together, always in secret. You know how I saw it? I saw it as if it was dirty, something dirty.... What there was between you and me was something dirty.

HE: I think you're going a bit far.

SHE: I'm not accusing you of anything. It's my fault. Everything got mixed up for me: living with my mother, the monotony.... I've had this sensation of starting to be grown up.... I don't know, it's like I'd run out of feelings, as if a part of me was dead, couldn't react.... So what peace do you want us to make?

HE: Let's go home.

10

SHE: I don't feel good about it all.

HE: Please.

SHE: I told you, I don't feel good.... It seems to me I have no feelings, for you or for anyone else. (*Referring to her work*) All there is is this. Do what I said I'd do, and do it whatever it takes. That's the only thing I really feel. (*She breaks away and tries to get back to work.*)

HE: OK! I'll help you for a while and then we'll go. (*He starts to help. Then, joking*) Which papers are these? Let's have a look.

SHE: (*Serious*) You know which papers they are.

HE: (*Pretending to make light of the situation*) You're going to hand them out, then?

Pause.

SHE: You don't think I should, do you?

HE: You know what I think about it. It's deliberately complicating things. And it's not the right time, either. There's too much shit going on to bring up an issue like this.

SHE: Exactly.

HE: I wouldn't do it now.

SHE: (*Ironically*) You've always been a bit too prudent, you have.

HE: Maybe so. But I reckon you know it'd be easier for me to say nothing and let you take a beating – tomorrow evening, when everyone's here.

SHE: Not everyone's going to be here.

HE: (*Losing patience*) Oh bollocks, I know. The delegates (*ironically*) and the lady delegates. As you wish, the members of the National Committee. But in practice, all of us will be here.... You can't just come out with accusations like these.

SHE: (*Calmly*) And why can't I?

HE: Well, first off because it's ingenuous. You'll be a total laughing stock if you don't have any proof.

SHE: What do you want, proof? Proof of what? I'm not talking about a crime. I'm questioning tendentious and manipulative behaviour by the people in charge. I'm questioning the lack of real leadership, the fact that a little coterie of mates are more concerned with keeping their cushy jobs than with what people need.

HE: You're wrong.

SHE: Where, where am I wrong? Don't we have a right to know if the work's being done along the political lines that were agreed? Or are we supposed to let everyone go off and do their own thing?

HE: (*Ironically*) Now I understand. Seeing as there's so many of us, and with the results from the last elections in front of us, what you want to do is create even more divisions...

SHE: I'm not making anything up.

HE: Listen, you and I have both dedicated our entire lives to this bloody party. I know things aren't going like they ought to, but there's a time for everything.

SHE: Are you trying to lecture me now?

HE: I'm not trying to lecture you, I just want you to see they're using you – someone's using you – and the people who look as if they're supporting you now, they don't actually believe in the position you're taking. And what's more, you're creating a difficult situation.

SHE: Difficult? For who? (*Pause.*) Mind you, you're not the first person who thinks so. Your friends have even got to the point of saying I'm making life difficult for you all...

HE: Up till now they were your friends too, as far as I know.

SHE: Look, you know what I think? All this being prudent makes me sick. I'm talking about hard facts, things that have happened, just like we say on these sheets of paper. And there are more still to come out. I want to know if the electoral lists are put together to pay off favours, in whatever way. And I want to know why the country hasn't discussed clearly what they promised would be done and hasn't been. We've got a right to ask questions, haven't we?

HE: Questions, yes, but there's a time for everything and this isn't the time.

SHE: And who decides when the time is right? Perhaps you can tell me?

HE: Why don't you calm down a bit?

SHE: Because I don't want to.... Let's talk straight. What are you trying to convince me of? Tell me the truth, have some balls, even if it's just for once in your life.

HE: But why are you treating me like this?

SHE: I'm not treating you like anything, I just want to know what it is you want.

HE: I've already told you what I want. It's very simple. I wanted for us to talk. I came to see you because I don't want to go on being the bad guy in this whole business. I don't want to see you buggered up because of me, and I don't want you to avoid me all the time, either.

SHE: What are you talking about now?

HE: I'm talking about you and me.

SHE: I don't understand. You turn up out of nowhere, I don't know what you're after.... You want us to say our relationship was all very nice and going fine, but now it doesn't matter? You want us to just forget the whole thing and be friends? You want us to leap into bed again when we have a spare moment? You want me to eat these papers? You want me to shut up? OK, but we've got to make a choice. One thing, or another. Whichever you want, but just the one. I'm too old not to know where I am...

HE: The way you put it...

SHE: I haven't finished.

Pause. SHE decides not to say anything; goes back to work, infuriated. HE watches her uneasily; walks around the stage. After a while, SHE speaks.

SHE: Go away, please. Go away and leave me alone. You shouldn't have come.

HE: The problem is I don't know what's going on with you. If I knew, I could...

SHE: You don't need to know anything about me, and I don't need to know anything about you. I just want to be on my own, on my own for once, and do what I feel like doing. And you don't need to play the nice man any more.

HE: I'm not playing the nice man...

SHE: Yes you are, and I'm the hysterical woman. And I don't like this distribution of roles.

HE: That's not it...

Pause. SHE doesn't listen, but lets him finish.

HE: What do you want me to say? That I'm sorry about what happened? Well, I'm very sorry about what happened, very. Maybe I did it all wrong. I was wound up, things weren't going well for me. We rowed. We talked and we rowed. And you were always saying we had to stop seeing each other.... We've always had too many rows, and now instead of sorting things out we're making life complicated and rowing again.... The fact is, I don't know where I am or what we're talking about.... Maybe it wasn't my fault, just...

SHE: OK, I've already said that. What else?

15

HE: What else? (*Unnerved*) I came to talk to you, to see if we could have a civilised relationship.

SHE: I really like civilised relationships, too. It's a polite way of saying you want to jump in the sack with me whenever you feel like it.

HE: Sod off!

SHE: (*Conciliatory*) Go away, please....

HE: All right, but tell me why we're arguing. And at least finish your work...

SHE: What's it matter?

Pause.

HE: Maybe that's the problem. It doesn't matter to you one way or the other. You're in a bad way and you don't want to admit it. And you've got this tendency to mix personal things with other things that aren't...

SHE: To mix personal things? (*Pause.*) I was preparing these papers which I have all the right in the world to distribute and...

HE: (*Approaching her*) I've come to make peace. Is it so difficult for you to understand that? There's still something between us, much as you try to hide it. I at least can tell you...

SHE: Don't be an arsehole.

HE tries to hold her, a little timidly at first, and then more boldly. SHE tries to resist, but hasn't the strength.

SHE: Let me go.

HE: (*Holding on to her*) Please....

SHE: (*Without energy*) Leave me alone. I don't want you to touch me.... What's all this play-acting leading to?

HE: I just told you I want to...

SHE: (*Scornfully*) You haven't told me anything.

HE: I told you I want to make our peace.

SHE: (*Shouting and pulling away from him*) I'm asking you to leave me alone.

HE: Don't shout.

SHE: Why? What are you afraid of? You afraid they'll hear us? Well I'm not. You come here, you threaten me...

HE: I'm not threatening you. I'm only asking you not to shout.

SHE: (*Shouting even more*) Well I want to shout. You hear me? I really feel like shouting. And I'll shout as much as I want, because the whole thing's a load of bullshit, complete bullshit.

HE: Please do me a favour and calm down.

SHE: (*Furious*) Who sent you here to talk to me?

HE: (*Surprised*) What are you talking about?

SHE: Who has sent you here to talk to me?

HE: No one's sent me anywhere.

SHE: You've come to persuade me not to say anything, not to present these papers, not to ask questions. You've come to tell me to shut up.

HE: You're making all this up, I suppose you realise that?

SHE: What is it I'm making up?

HE: I found out you were still here in the theatre and I thought it was a good time to talk.

SHE: You've already said that.

HE: You're making enemies without any need to.

SHE: And what the fuck does it matter to you?

HE: It does matter to me, that's why I've come, because I don't want you doing things you're going to regret later on.

SHE: (*Making an obvious effort to calm herself*) Let me think for a moment. Now I'm the one asking you not to go. You're right about one thing, we're mixing things up. But it's you who's doing it, not me.

HE tries to speak.

SHE: No, shut up, shut up until I've finished. What is it I'm doing wrong? The fact that I don't want to take any more shit? Is that what I'm doing wrong? Can't you understand that I need to feel clean? Clean. I can't live if everything around me is rotten and it's all lies.

HE: You're seeing things which just aren't there.

SHE: So I'm going crazy, am I?

HE: (*Makes as if to leave*) That's enough childishness.

SHE: Didn't you say you'd come to talk to me? Now I'm asking you, please, will you stay? I won't shout. I just would like to clear a few things up. If you say I'm mistaken, that means you think I'm doing something wrong. What is it?

HE: I told you. You're looking for problems where they're not. You'll hurt a lot of people.

Pause.

SHE: Wait. Where do I get this power from?

HE: What power?

SHE: If I can cause so much hurt like you say, that means I have power. Where do I get this power from?

HE: You're beginning to scare me a bit.

SHE: And you me. You know I thought for a minute you wanted to take me off to bed. I was angry, and God knows how, when you touched me the woman I thought was dead came back again. I could see myself stuck to you again,

19

always hanging on your whims. Then I thought you wanted to collect up what was left of me so you could have a little roll in the hay. Maybe I'd even have liked that. At least you made me feel something.

HE again makes as if to leave. SHE holds him by the arm with some violence, and stops him.

HE: Let me go.

It isn't clear whether they hate or desire each other.

SHE: Look, these papers aren't important at all now. You were so scared of them and now they're nothing. And what I thought had brought you here isn't anything either. Aren't you interested in my body anymore? Aren't you interested at all? I thought you were, that it still excited you, like before. I thought that was the most important thing between us. Touching each other, us having each other. I'm sorry I thought that, obviously. But now I'm starting to see where we are.

HE: (*Trying to leave*) I'm going.

SHE: (*Holding him back*) No, don't go. Not yet. You've got to listen to me, and I'll do whatever it takes for you to stay. What do you want? (*She lifts up her skirt*) Is this what you want? The truth is I wouldn't mind either. I need to feel something, I need to know I'm still alive.

HE pushes her away.

HE: Please.

SHE: (*Touching him*) I'm all right, don't be afraid. I haven't lost my senses, or anything resembling them. I won't shout. I just want you to stay. When you arrived I had no desire to fuck you. I don't know how to say it. I wanted to believe I didn't feel like it and never would again. But it turns out I was wrong.

HE: That's enough.

SHE: (*Insisting*) What are you afraid of? Are you afraid someone's going to come? Everyone knows you and I used to see each other. I've told a few people myself – not many, but everyone knows. And you've said it yourself: yeah, that one, I shag her whenever I want....

HE: (*Breaking away, violently*) I said that's enough!

SHE: (*Shouting*) Well tell me then, where does this power you say I've got come from?

HE: I asked you not to shout.

SHE: (*Quieter*) Where does this power you say I've got come from?

HE: I don't understand, I don't know what you're talking about.

SHE: Yes you do know.

HE: I swear, I'm very sorry I came, I didn't want to hurt you at all. Forgive me....

SHE: You're full of shit, and a liar. You did it before, the hurt, when I clung to you like a child. Maybe I took things too much to heart, didn't understand it was different for you. It amused you that I thought what we had was serious, didn't it?

HE: It didn't amuse me at all, and when I ended our relationship I wasn't aware of hurting you so much either. What more can I say?

SHE: You weren't aware? You didn't realise I'd stuck to you because I was alone, feeling like a piece of shit, they'd destroyed me, hadn't even left me air to breathe? You didn't see you were the only thing I had left? I was sincere, but you used me without a second thought, and then later, when it suited you, you got rid of me. 'Goodbye. I'm too old for you, there's nothing I can offer you. I've got a family....' It was all lies.

HE: Things didn't happen the way you're telling them.

SHE: You bastard.... And when you told me passionately how you enjoyed making love with me, how you didn't want to lose me, was that all a lie too?

HE: I was telling you the truth. I swear I was telling you the truth.

SHE: No.

HE: I was telling you the truth. But you can't always do what you want.

SHE: I understand now. You were telling me the truth when you had it up inside me, and when you took it out you changed your mind. That's very human. It's the way things go, isn't it?

HE: It's best if I go.

SHE: Maybe it is. But I feel bad about you going without understanding me properly. (*Pause.*) I knew you didn't want things to get too complicated – I understood that. I was prepared to do anything, go on the way you told me things had to be, for as long as it took. But I didn't want to be just another one you shagged when you felt like it. (*Pause.*) You see, I wasn't asking for much, but it turns out that overnight you weren't interested in me anymore. You turned the whole thing around. It was you who was suffering, you who had the really big problems we needed to understand. And it was us other people who had to make the sacrifices. If I wanted to go on I had to accept your new rules. Because you're strong, you're powerful, you're a man. And you finished it. You just went.

HE: That's enough of that.

SHE: Yes, you're right. It happened, OK. Right, that's that, sorted. In the end we adults have to get used to being on our own and put up with everyone else's failings. I must have been made for it. Life's a pile of shit, we know that. All this stuff happens to loads of people – it's no big deal. But the fact is, you never get used to people treating you wrong. You always aspire to a bit of luck. You always think things'll go a bit better for you. But then they don't. For you, things didn't turn out too well in the end. Now you're...

HE: You're manipulating it all. No way was the basis of our relationship ever like you're saying.

SHE: Ah! So our relationship had a basis?

HE: I give up. You win. I've always been deceitful, I'm a bad person, I had a specific interest in hurting you, I made up all those problems, I never had any feelings for you. I don't know what else to say.

SHE throws some of the papers on the floor; rummages through the bag on the back of the chair, seemingly looking for a pack of cigarettes. Eventually she finds one, semi-crushed. HE looks at her, then begins picking up the papers from the floor.

SHE: Leave all that.

HE: I don't mind.

SHE: (*Shouting*) I want you to leave it alone!

HE raises his hands momentarily, showing he is leaving it.

HE: When you get like this you're impossible.

SHE: What's impossible for you is anything which runs contrary to your own ideas. Be it with left-wingers, or your cock. You're the man.

HE: Things don't all have to be black or white.

SHE lights her cigarette.

SHE: Tell me something. Nothing's going to happen, I won't shout, I won't get hysterical.... Tell me who sent you to talk to me.

HE: I've already told you: no one. I thought if we made up and could talk, perhaps your attitude wouldn't be so... I don't know... I don't want to start all over again....

SHE: Neither do I, but I want to know the truth.

HE: (*Uncertain*) I just wanted to avoid you making a mistake with the people in the party.

SHE: I don't know if I can talk about the people in the party.

HE: That's what it's about.

SHE: And you've come to ask me, on behalf of some of them, not to take the lid off anything.

HE: That's what I am asking, but it's not because of what you think it is.

SHE: Explain to me.

HE: You know the reasons.... Your contribution might not be expedient.

SHE: I don't quite understand. (*Pause.*) You've agreed to exploit our relationship to defend a bunch of slimeballs who only see politics in terms of their own self-interest?

HE: I haven't agreed anything. But you know what I mean. You need to know what they're saying.

SHE: Are you that downtrodden?

HE: It's not how you think.

SHE: But what are you afraid of?

HE: Of what you're getting ready, of these papers. All that. That's what I'm afraid of.

SHE: But this is nothing.

HE: You've got them worried.

SHE: They pretend to be. There's a bit of a game behind all this: if they don't pretend I'm important, then they aren't either.

HE: That's not quite how it is. And maybe you haven't thought through enough what might happen if you say what I think you're going to say.

SHE: And you have?

HE: What I mean is...

SHE: What you mean is I'm acting blindly, no idea what I'm doing, as usual. (*Ironically*) Perhaps I'm not as close as you are to all the internal wrangling, but I'm perfectly aware of the situation.

HE: They could make life very difficult for you.

SHE: For me?

HE: Yes, for you.

SHE: And why is that, may I ask?

HE: Well, because no one likes being buggered about with.

SHE: But didn't we say this was an open project, everyone could have their say, and that only out of sincere debate would a new type of politics emerge?

HE: There are elements in the party who do not always understand certain approaches.

SHE: Which elements are these?

HE: The unions, for example.

SHE: That's enough playing the union card.

HE: I don't know how to make you see...

SHE: You don't need to make me see anything.

HE: I think I do, I have a certain right.

SHE: You have a certain what?

HE: It's a manner of speech.

SHE: It's a crap manner of speech.

HE: OK, it's a crap manner of speech, but I've got to make you see...

SHE: Here we go again. You've always been a macho bastard. 'I have a right,' 'I've got to make you see,' 'I'm concerned about you.'

HE: Who's delivering the sermons now?

Pause. They look at each other. HE approaches SHE. He tries to stroke her head.

HE: Please.

SHE: Leave me alone. I want you to leave me alone.

HE insists. Eventually, SHE appears to give in.

HE: You know what? When it comes down to it I don't give a toss about all this. I just want peace and quiet. With you. Like the best times. We ought to be able to put aside all this shit that's screwing us up.

SHE: So the party's shit, then?

HE: No, no it isn't, but I'm tired, I've had enough.

SHE: I'm not as strong as I seem, either.

HE: I know.

Tenderly, HE takes her face in his hands, and looks at her. SHE closes her eyes.

HE: Let's go to your place.

SHE: I can't.

HE touches her forehead, her hair, a cheek. Then SHE lets him put his arms round her waist, and he kisses her gently on the lips, once, twice, three times.

HE: It's a shame.

SHE also kisses him, perhaps more passionately than he did, but she is nervous.

SHE: I want you, but we can't.

HE: Come here.

HE runs his hands over her body and then begins to slowly undo her clothes. SHE strokes his face. HE hugs her tightly, slowly. Then he puts his hands on her breasts. SHE pulls away a little.

SHE: No, not here, those people might come in.

HE: Let's go to one of the dressing rooms.

SHE: No, please. We can't.

HE: Why not?

SHE: Now isn't the time.

HE: Why isn't now the time?

SHE: I just can't see all this.

HE: (*Touching her*) What is it you don't see?

SHE: Us, the fighting, everything.

HE: Let's go home. We'll talk...

SHE: (*Trying to free herself from him*) No, no it's not right. It'd be the same thing over again.

HE: (*Not letting her go*) I don't want us to argue again. And I don't want to lose you, either. I really mean it.

SHE: We're not going to argue.

HE: (*Hugging her*) You know what? If we'd thought more about ourselves we wouldn't be like this now. (*Pause.*) You as well as I have been thinking too much about other people. I've been keeping out of the way too much, and you always face up to them.

SHE: You've got to understand that I can't just give up on what I think is right. It's all I have left.

HE: (*Seemingly joking*) Not even if I ask you to?

SHE: I'm talking seriously here.

HE: So am I.

SHE: Well, it seems like you're taking the piss.

HE: (*Impatiently*) No, but we haven't got all day, either. It's tomorrow, you know.

SHE: (*Pulling away from him a little*) Are you getting in a hurry?

HE: No, but...

SHE: I don't believe you. You're not telling me the truth now, either.

HE: I have told you the truth.

SHE: You haven't told me anything at all. You've given me a good grope, got me a bit excited – you know about that. Great. But now I want to know what it is you get out of convincing me to leave things be.

HE: I don't get anything, I swear.

SHE: They've got you by the balls, I can see.

HE: I'm convinced of what I'm doing.

SHE: They've promised you something. They told you, 'You go, you know her well, you used to shag her.' (*Pause.*) You know, I actually feel a bit sorry for you. And it looks as if you've come here for nothing.

HE: You've got no right to talk to me like that.

SHE: And getting your hands on me again, was that part of the job they gave you to do?

HE: That's enough, please.

SHE: Now I'm not sure if you wanted to fuck me or if it was just a work thing.

HE: It was you who got me going.

SHE: (*Feigning surprise*) Oh, you're right. I hadn't realised. I got you going. (*Performing the actions she describes*) I came up to you like this, I rubbed my belly against your crotch, then you put your hands on my breasts and we snogged. (*Making as if to kiss him, then pulling away.*) You don't know how much you disgust me.

HE: Nobody gave me the job of coming to see you. I know myself what needs doing. OK, you want to know if we've talked about it? Well, yes we have. We've talked about it. We've talked about you, and your stubborn obsession with stirring up things.

SHE: At last. At last we have the truth. You've talked about it.

HE: You've known it all the time, right from the very first moment.

SHE: Right from the very first moment.... Maybe I have.

HE: You wanted to see if I was capable of convincing you. I couldn't do it. Maybe you're right when you say I'm getting past it and they've got me by the balls. You, on the other hand, had no doubt at all. As soon as you saw me here you knew what I was up to. Then things got mixed up.

SHE: Things got mixed up.

HE: Yes.

SHE: How vulgar you are.

HE: Vulgar?

SHE: Yes, vulgar. Perhaps you're not aware of that.

HE: Leave the stories. Trading insults'll get us nowhere. Better talking straight.

SHE: I assure you I couldn't be straighter. You don't understand my motives, do you? And you don't understand either, nor have you ever understood, my feelings. I'll tell you again: there is nothing more important in my life right now than telling all of you that underneath the big concepts you use there is nothing, absolutely nothing, there's just all of you and your poor personal miseries. I'm not saying that's how it always is. I'm saying that, in this case, that's how it is. And let me just tell you one more thing: nothing will happen. You have more strength, you do, and you move slowly, you wait for the most favourable moment. That's what you call being politicians.

HE: You're letting yourself get carried away with words.

SHE: Me?

HE: Yes, and you haven't got even the slightest notion of what it is to be practical – you never have done. You've been going on and on to me about the great sacrifices you've made since we met, and you know what? Me, I've got severe problems in my life. Specific problems that I can't sort out, and I have to carry on, whether I like it or I don't like it. And, as well as that, it so happens I've dedicated many years to this collective which, like all others, has its problems, contradictions and difficulties, but to get along with others one has to have a certain sense of when's the right time. And you haven't got it, not with me and not with the party. You always have to be the most honest one, the one who makes the most sacrifices, and, of course, the one who demands most.... You know what? Maybe the other women who've been round to my place weren't as good a fuck as you, but they weren't half as much of a pain in the arse.

SHE: We're hurting ourselves again.

HE: (*Cynically*) No, not at all. It's good. All of this had to come out. You always do the same thing, you take advantage of an argument to throw back in my face things I've said to you when I've lost my rag. We fight, we fuck, we fight, we fuck.

SHE: Not this time.

HE: No, not this time.

Pause.

SHE: Tomorrow I'm going to feel like shit, but now I'm starting to see things more clearly. I want to be calm, very calm. Now, thanks to you, I can bury that woman who felt broken, precisely because we only fought and fucked. In fact, you know what the real problem is? When you and I got together I was already dead and you just didn't realise it. At least I'd rather believe you didn't realise instead of having to admit you played with me. And that explains our relationship.

HE: I don't know what you're talking about.

SHE: No, of course you don't. I've given you everything, and you've given me nothing.

SHE sits down, slowly, and puts her head in her hands; takes a deep breath and straightens up as best she can. Next, she runs her finger-tips round her eyes, and then rests her hands on her legs. She lets her hair down and combs her fingers through it as if that will restore her. She puts her head back and closes her eyes. HE smokes, and looks at her. SHE, having recovered her composure a little, appears to look for cigarettes. She doesn't find any. HE throws her a packet. SHE takes it without speaking, and calmly takes out a cigarette, lights it, and smokes. SHE gets up and goes to the table.

34

HE: What do you think you'll do?

SHE: About what?

HE: Listen...

SHE: I would like you to leave.

SHE starts to work again on the papers, stapling them noisily. HE watches her for a few seconds.

HE: I'll put it another way. I need you to help me. If I go back and tell them I haven't been able to persuade you.... I have no idea what to do. Can't you understand that?

SHE carries on working, without speaking.

HE: Think about it for a moment. I'm not asking you to do anything outrageous. Let them fight it out among themselves. Don't get caught up in it. You and I can start again. Time has moved on, I see things differently now.

SHE: Stop.

HE: You know where you and I went wrong? That both of us take things too much to heart. If I'd been able to take no notice of the others...

SHE: I said stop.

HE: No. Listen, I mean it. I want us to get back together.

SHE: Every time you open your mouth you make a bigger fool of yourself.

HE: You see me as some kind of scumbag, don't you? You think I'm contemptible. You accuse me of everything, you say I haven't got any feelings...

SHE: I haven't said anything like that, but you're making it very easy for me.

HE: OK, as you wish. But I think you're the one who's making such a big deal of personal grudges. Obviously we're not going to understand each other if you're prepared to go ahead without considering who you hurt...

SHE: I think you're the one getting carried away with words.

HE: These people you despise have made more sacrifices than you, and they have more right than you to...

SHE: And that means they're allowed to deceive us? First you were Marxists, then you were Socialists, and ecologists, feminists, nationalists, Europeans... why don't you say once and for all that the ideology, the programme, everything you say in the newspapers, is false, false, completely false. You have the time of your bloody lives and you'd change the whole lot from top to bottom just so a handful of people can keep hold of their personal privileges?

HE: You want us to believe that if we acted in another way, everything would be different. Nothing works like that, anywhere, and you ought to know that. It is, if you like, contemptible, but we know of no other system, and neither you, nor I, nor anyone has any possibility of changing the world.

SHE: You all go around saying yes you can.

HE: Not in the way you imply.

SHE: Now I can see that we have nothing in common. Maybe we've never had anything in common.

HE: Or maybe what we had, however much or little that was, you've destroyed.

SHE: You're not going to trick me again. What happened a moment ago is nothing to you, is it?

HE: I like you, you know that.

SHE: And nothing more, obviously.

HE: You're way over the top. Why do you want to make things complicated for me like that?

SHE: I don't want to complicate anything. I just want you to admit that you're finished, you've let yourself be overrun and you're prepared to do anything.

HE: I've already told you that. I told you I've got nowhere to hide and I need you. But maybe I can still do more damage than you think.

SHE: Are you threatening me now?

HE: No... but our personal history's got nothing to do with what you're planning to do tomorrow night. I don't know why you obstinately insist on mixing the two things up.

SHE: Can I remind you it was you who came looking for a reconciliation?

HE: I came because I wanted to talk to a grown-up woman.

SHE: And you found a tired, empty person with no illusions.

HE: I found a little woman with a grudge who can't see beyond her feelings, who confuses personal life with that of a group of people, and what's more doesn't realise what's happening to me.

SHE: Right. That's what you found.

HE: And I also found a fellow party member who for some time has been throwing spanners in the works without anticipating the consequences of what she's doing. I tell you sincerely, you can't always knock other people, and you can't discredit our proposals without knowing them...

SHE: (*Referring to the papers*) But all of this is nothing! Nothing! All of you are giving me an importance I haven't got.

Pause.

HE: (*Also referring to the papers*) Leave it. We've all had a bad screw.

SHE: What'd you say?

HE: What I said...

SHE: No, it's not all your fault... I need to rescue myself on my own. If I want my life to have any meaning I need to say what I think... I need to do something. Don't you understand? There comes a time when you have to say that's enough.

HE: Think again. If you dig up too much shit they'll crush me to pieces. If you want, I promise you...

SHE: You promise me? What? I'm talking about something else. The woman has been unlucky, the friend is tired, the militant lost her energy.... All there is left is me, and I don't want to be ashamed of myself... I can't take any more lies.

HE: What lies?

SHE: Not yours, not mine. But I can see you don't understand.... All right. I accept that you believe in it. I accept that you are sincere. I accept that you need me, whatever.... But the truth is that nothing of what you say is how you say it is...

HE: That's enough of that. You yourself say it's not so important.

SHE: Yes it is, I can see that now. But its not about illegal funding or anything that's going to put us in prison. I'm talking about the lies we've told ourselves, how we've changed, the quantity of stuff we've had to swallow. We've attacked honesty. You see? Honesty, seems quite an old word, doesn't it? Well, that's what we've done: we've stopped being honest. That's important, you know.

HE: You'll cause splits.

SHE: So what?

HE: So what? Maybe there's something you want in exchange for keeping quiet?

SHE looks at him, surprised.

HE: Everyone wants something, don't look at me like that. And if you don't want anything, then I'm even more mistaken about you. It means you're just a person with a grudge.

SHE: I prefer to say that I'm a person who is hurt, very hurt.

HE: In any event it hasn't got anything to do with what we have to decide.

SHE: It has got something to do with it, but I can understand that for you it seems empty and demagogic...

HE: Say what you want, we haven't got time.

SHE: People like me don't want anything. I've already told you. And what's more you can't give me anything either. I feel alone... as if I were on a black beach, battered by wind. I'm tired that everything has to make you laugh, everything has to be a joke, everything has to be empty and false, everything has to be dirty.

HE: Fine, but I need to know what you're going to do tomorrow.

SHE: But if it doesn't matter...

HE: That's not true. For us it's important.

SHE: (*Staring at him*) OK, look then, tomorrow I will do what I think is best: I will say the truth, and what's more I will denounce the contradictions in what you call the project, I will say that ten, twenty or thirty of you have turned yourselves into a mafia, I'll say how you put people on the electoral lists, I'll explain how you use institutions to your personal benefit, I'll make you talk about the public money that indirectly ends up in the party. And by the by, I'll also have to define you in terms of things, maybe just invented to get into the papers, but that you're often messing about with: the country, the language, ideological coherence.... And what I'm looking for, I've already told you this, is for me to feel as clean as I possibly can. Perhaps you're right to suppose I have a certain power. And you know where I get it from? From the fact that I have nothing to lose. I aspire to nothing, I ask for nothing, I want nothing from anyone. However, the others, you yourself...

HE: You've lost your senses.

SHE: Maybe I have. But now I don't know how I can live if I can't see the difference between good and bad. (*Pause.*) I know you'll win, but at least it'll be clear that with the way you justify yourselves nothing new can be built...

HE: You'll do a lot of people damage, and there's no future in that.

HE goes up to her and, in a final attempt, puts his hand on her back.

HE: Listen...

SHE: (*Infuriated*) Don't touch me.

HE: You're wrong, it's impossible to work from a basis solely of disillusionment.

SHE: No, I'm not wrong. The only thing that counts is if you've done what you thought was best.

HE: Even if you harm other people?

SHE: Don't make me laugh.... You know what I regret about all this? That you and I have got hurt. In the end, only people should count.

HE: You don't know what you're talking about.

SHE: Yes I do.

HE wavers, and finally leaves. SHE goes back to work. STAGE-HAND appears.

STAGEHAND: Sorry, where do you want these flags?

CURTAIN.

Naked

Joan Casas

First performed at Teatre Poliorama, Barcelona
21 January 1993

Cast:

She – Mercé Lleixá
He – Manel Barceló

Creative Team:

Director
Set Design – Ramon Siró

Produced by the Centre Dramátic de la Generalitat

Translated into English by Peter Bush

SINGLE ACT

A man in his thirties – nothing out of the ordinary. A woman in her thirties – nothing out of the ordinary. They are wearing light, summer clothes.

A house attic. We can see the sloping structure of the roof. Entry is through a trapdoor in the floor and it's open. Left front is a wing-backed armchair, its stuffing hanging out. Next to a standard lamp, its shade and fitting dangling awkwardly from the electric cable. Right back is a trunk. Front right, a naked bulb attached to a wall or high beam. Left back, a big skylight comes down to the floor. At the beginning, it is covered by a shutter and everything is dark. Centre back, an extended screen. Behind the screen, out of sight, is a mattress.

The trapdoor opens and a little light comes in from beneath. SHE climbs up and in. HE, for the moment, just sticks his head through. SHE crouches down by his head and points to the space: the attic.

HE: (*Looking though the trapdoor*) You know? It's a nice house, but it feels empty. Not very lived in. In fact you feel it's been a long time since anybody lived here. And it makes no difference if a cleaning woman comes once a week. That probably makes it even worse. As if week after week her cloth and broom erased the traces of the living, made them even colder. You know what I mean?

SHE: Yes, perhaps.

HE: It's strange you have a house like this and never come here.

SHE: Hardly ever really.

HE: If it were mine, I'd be here all the time. You know, I'm sure I wouldn't be what I'm like now, if I lived here. I mean place is important; the decor changes us.

SHE: We are the decor.

HE: Right, if you look at it that way...

SHE: And I like you as you are. (*She stands up.*) Come on, what do you think?

HE: About the attic? Christ, what do you expect me to think? (*He's climbed in and is sitting on the top of the ladder, his feet hanging through the hole.*)

SHE: It's my little hideaway.

HE: When I was a kid I dreamed about having a house with an attic. It's like a space where you can keep your secrets, right? At least, I always imagined secrets there, the things that are always kept there, like old clothes, or toys abandoned in a dusty trunk full, in one corner of the attic... a trunk like this. Citizen Kane's sleigh – Orson Welles, 'Rosebud'. Remember that image? Well, you know what I mean. But we lived in a flat. We didn't have at attic at home.

SHE: You are disappointed then.

HE: No. Maybe it's a touch empty. I'm not sure. It's dark. I can't see much.

SHE: Wait a minute. If that's the case.... (*Walks to the left and disappears into a dark corner.*)

46

Prolonged silence.

HE: Where've you got to? What've you done with yourself? (*Pause. No reply.*) Light a match, don't go on like this. (*Pause.*) You must have a lighter....(*Pause.*) Hey, can't you hear me? (*Long pause. He stands up, takes two steps. The trapdoor suddenly closes. Everything is dark.*) If it's one of your little jokes, I don't think it's very funny. (*Pause.*) All right. What's the game? You want to frighten me? (*Moves and stumbles into something.*) Shit, I've bloody hurt myself now!

The bulb on the right lights up and gives out a very feeble light. SHE emerges from the half dark on the left, by the armchair, carrying an object we can't see and which she puts on the floor, out of his sight.

SHE: What's the matter?

HE: I stumbled.

SHE: You went all quiet.

HE: I'm hardly to blame. I don't like the dark. It stresses me out!

SHE: You poor thing.

HE: All right. You couldn't care a fuck. Ouch, it hurts! I want to see what the damage is. I bumped into this. I've hurt myself.

SHE: Yes, I heard.

HE: What's this box then? Your treasure-chest? (*Pause.*) I reckon I've drawn blood. I want to have a look. (*Rolls up his trouser leg.*)

47

SHE: Go on then. (*Sits in the armchair.*)

HE: You see? I thought as much. I must have done it with one of these metal clasps. Or on this hinge that's half off. It's ripped my trousers and blood's trickling. It's only a scratch but it's the shinbone and very painful. (*Pause.*) You know what you should do now, don't you? Come here, wet the wound with your saliva and breathe on it. Isn't that what you did when you were a kid? (*Pause.*) Come on, why not?

SHE: No.

HE: You frightened of blood? (*Pause.*) I can't bend down that far to breathe on it! (*Pause.*) All right, I'll come to you. (*Gets up.*)

SHE: No, don't move.

HE: What do you mean 'don't move'?

SHE: That you shouldn't move.

HE: Listen, what's got into you? (*Pause.*) Do we always have to stay a long way from each other? I like having you next to me.

SHE: And I like looking at you from here.

Pause.

HE: Can't you switch this standard lamp on? Is it broken?

SHE: No, it works.

HE: So why don't you switch it on? You've got a good view of me but I can hardly see you. It's not fair. The wings of the armchair cast a shadow over your face. And I can't see your lips. I don't know if you're in a serious mood, like you were before. (*Pause.*) No, I bet you aren't, I bet you're smiling, those teeth of yours with the little gaps in between that I like so much. (*Brief pause.*) Or maybe you're laughing, or crying. Why don't you switch the light on?

SHE: It's OK as it is.

HE: In fact, I reckon you're laughing at me. Are you laughing at me? (*Pause.*) Because I stumbled so stupidly. I must look laughable, with my trouser leg rolled up and a sock round my ankle. (*Pause.*) I know why you don't want me to come near you. It's because of what happened downstairs a minute ago, isn't it? (*Pause.*) I've said I'm sorry once. Do you want me to say it again? I'm too hot-headed at times, I know. But when you told me to stop, I stopped, didn't I? (*Pause.*) What do you expect me to do? You're as much to blame. You know I like you, don't you? And today I saw something in your eyes I'd not seen before. They were glinting as if they were wet. It wasn't at all as if you'd been crying. I don't quite know how to say this, but you were looking at me in a way that made me think...

SHE: Shut up.

HE: We were alone, we're adults, we know what we want. (*Pause.*) Because you want or wanted it or apparently did. (*Pause.*) You didn't say a word when I put my hand on you. (*Pause.*) The fact is you never say a word. And you were looking at me like that. Suddenly you went so quiet, that I don't know what came over me.... (*Pause.*) But that's past history now. I think I've apologised. But I can do so again if you like. Would you like me to kneel down? (*He kneels.*)

SHE: Shut up. Take your shirt off.

HE: What's that?

SHE: I said: take your shirt off.

HE: Hey, lady, if I do the stripper bit you can provide the music. Whistling. That's just what I wanted to hear.

SHE: Please. I like looking at you. I told you I did.

HE: (*Pause. Gets up.*) Right you are. (*Starts to unbutton.*) Whatever you say. However you want me. You want me to take my shirt off? I'll take my shirt off. (*Takes it off, is naked from the waist up.*) Is that OK for you?

SHE: Now take your trousers off.

HE: This is absurd. (*Sits on the trunk, puts his shirt down next to him. Starts to unlace a shoe.*)

SHE: What are you doing now?

HE: (*Curtly*) I'm unlacing my shoes. Don't you want me to take my trousers off? First I must take my shoes off. My trousers won't slip over my shoes. Why are you laughing?

SHE: Can't I laugh? If you could see yourself....

HE: I know I look absurd. This whole situation is absurd. (*Pulls a shoe off and bounces it on the floor.*) Are you sure there's

50

no broken glass on the floor? Or nails? A nail through the foot is just what I need. (*Bounces the other shoe on the floor. Stands up and unzips his trousers.*) You wanted my trousers off too? There you are. (*Drops them, first takes one foot out, then the other, puts his trousers next to his shirt. He's down to his pants and socks.*) Satisfied? Can I get dressed now?

SHE: No, no, and no again. I like looking at you.

HE: Hey? Do you think I've got fat? That'll do, won't it? (*Silence.*) Don't you think that's enough? (*Silence.*) It's cold up here. I'll put my shirt back on. (*Picks up his shirt.*)

SHE: No! (*Pause.*) Please don't. Not yet. It's not doing any harm, is it?

HE: Any harm? None at all. But it doesn't make any sense. It's ridiculous. It's absurd. I feel.... (*Sits on the trunk, puts his shirt down again.*) What an idiot! I was going to say I feel stark naked. Hear what I said? Do you think it's funny? Well? At least let me see your face! I can't stand not being able to see your face!

Pause. SHE lights a cigarette. The flame from the lighter momentarily lights up her face in the shadow from the sides of the armchair.

SHE: Here I am. I'm looking at you.

HE: I know. I know you're here. I know you're looking at me. But it's as if you were on the moon and looking at me through a telescope. (*Pause. He starts to take his socks off.*) If they had newspapers on the moon, I can imagine the head-lines: 'Earth-people don't have black feet!' 'Big discovery! Not all earth-people have black feet. Some cover them with a kind of wrap you can take off. And that often have

51

holes in them.' (*Pause.*) The smell doesn't carry to the moon, right? (*Pause.*) You sure there's no broken glass? (*Pause. Puts his feet on the floor.*) But there is lots of dust. They'll get filthy. Can I have a cigarette? (*He gets up, starts to go over to her.*)

SHE: No need to move, here.... (*Throws him the packet.*) The lighter.... (*Throws him the lighter.*) I don't want you to move.

HE: All right. I get you. You over there and me, over here. I get you. (*Lights a cigarette, sits down again.*) And I was thinking... thinking we'd get really close today. (*Pause.*) That you were bringing me so we could fuck, I mean! What did you expect me to think? (*Pause.*) To get back to where I was: as if you were on the moon. Or as if you were standing over me in a white coat and with a microscope. As if you were looking at me through a microscope. It's the same distancing effect.

SHE: I feel you're really close.

HE: Oh, you do, do you?

SHE: Increasingly so.

HE: That's funny. I still feel as I'm taking items of clothing off. Or you're the one taking them off, I'm not sure. One after another. I thought stripping was easy., and it turns out it isn't.

SHE: No.

HE: Lapidary. The voice of wisdom. (*Pause.*) When you deign to break your silence, it's as if you speak with the voice of wisdom. You don't waste a word. On the other

52

hand, I speak just for the sake of it. Because I've got a mouth and I ramble on and on, I know. Silence stresses me out. Silence when I'm with someone, when I'm with you. I need to fill them up. I feel there's only a very thin piece of string between us, a slender thread. And that all of a sudden I'll be alone, thinking I'm not alone. (*Changes tone.*) Aren't you scared of the silence? Of course you're not. You're the queen of silence. Extract a word from your lips is like I don't know what. And in the meantime, I rabbit on, about God, the devil, or whatever. Just so I can look into your eyes and see you're listening to me, then know I'm alive, that I'm alive because of you, that I've got weight, density. (*Pause.*) But for the moment I can't see your eyes.

She: I love you.

HE silently finishes his cigarette, throws the fag-end on the floor. SHE throws hers down and crushes it underfoot. HE takes a shoe and crushes his, then stands up.

HE: My pants?

SHE: Yes, please.

HE: (*Takes off his pants, stands naked in front of the trunk, striking a vaguely statuesque pose, looking at the audience.*) That do you?

SHE: You clown. (*Picks up the object she'd put down by the side of the armchair.*)

HE: You're right. (*Relaxes his stance, looks in her direction.*)

SHE: Keep still. For a second. (*The object is a Polaroid camera with a flash.*) That's right. Don't move. (*She takes a photograph of him.*)

HE: Are you mad? What are you up to now? (*Picks up his pants and puts them back on. Goes over to her and grabs the photo that's coming out of the camera.*) Give me that. (*Looks at the photo, standing by the armchair.*) Now you can see it clearer. (*Keeps looking as the image takes shape.*) What an odd feeling. Am I like this? Really? (*Pause.*) I can see it's me obviously. But I think I look odd. I don't know how to describe it. Like a model at art school. I went to art school for a while. Did I ever tell you? The first day we had a life-class we got very excited. The whole lot of us. A naked model and us all dressed, don't know what went on in our heads. But after ten minutes we looked at that girl, who was very pretty, as if she were a lump of plaster. You can believe that, I expect. (*Pause.*) Do you look at me and think: a lump of plaster?

She: No.

HE: So why did you do that?

SHE: I just thought of it.

HE: Just thought of it? You must be kidding! You made your mind up when we came up here.

SHE: Yes.

HE: (*Half shocked, half annoyed*) You set this all up. (*Goes to the trunk, puts the photo next to his clothes. Picks his shirt up and puts it on without buttoning it up.*) What was the point of all this? What were you trying to prove?

SHE: Nothing at all.

HE: Was it your revenge?

HE: For what?

HE: (*Points to the trunk*) What's inside there?

She: Open it.

HE releases the catch and lifts the lid. It's an effort but it finally opens all at once. The trousers, socks and photo, that were on top, slide down behind the trunk.

HE: My clothes will be all creased now. This attic has never seen a broom. (*Pause. Looks inside.*) No sign of Orson Welles's sleigh. There's just a stack of paper. Comics, books, school exercise books. Lots of school exercise books. (*He takes one out.*) Are they yours?

She: Some are.

HE: This one is. It's got your name in it. On a sticker with little flowers. (*Sniffs the book.*)

SHE: What are you doing?

HE: Old paper's got a very special smell.

SHE: Silly.

HE: Do you know your handwriting was very pretty? Mine was a disaster. And my exercise books were always full of crossings-out. (*Reads. Lets slip a laugh.*)

She: What's making you laugh?

HE: It's a composition. Do you want me to read it to you?

It's called 'A Lie'. It begins like this: 'It's very bad to tell lies, and that's why I never tell any.' How old were you? Ten? Nine?

SHE: I don't remember.

HE: Is it true you never lie?

SHE: Never.

HE: Now will you let me come over to you?

SHE: No, not really.

HE: (*Offering a cigarette*) Do you want one?

SHE: No, but give them back to me.

HE: No. Not if you don't want a smoke. (*Puts them in his pocket.*) You smoke too much. (*Goes over to the window and struggles with the catch.*) Doesn't this window open?

SHE: No.

HE: And this light? You said it worked, didn't you? How does it light?

SHE: Screw the bulb in.

HE screws the bulb and the light comes on. The bulb is more powerful than the one on the other side. HE and SHE look at each other in silence.

HE: You're odd, you know? (*Pause.*) But no more than I am. You tell me what I'm doing here like this. (*Pause. Points at the way he's dressed.*) Do you really love me?

56

She: Yes.

HE: I know you do. I don't know why I ask. You never tell lies.

HE crouches down and takes the Polaroid, is going to take a photo of her. SHE calmly puts a hand in front of her face.

SHE: No. (*Pause.*) No, there's no need.

HE: (*Puts the camera to one side, but keeps hold of it*) There's no need? You know Indians in America didn't like having their photos taken. They said the camera stole their shadows from them. They said buffaloes became extinct because the white men started to draw and photograph them. (*Puts the camera on the floor.*) You really are stark naked. And always have been. (*Slowly, in front of her, starts taking his shirt and pants off again. He puts his clothes on the floor.*) I find it hard.

SHE: Shush.

HE: The Indians were more afraid of cameras than of guns. Guns kill our bodies, they said, but cameras take our souls away.

SHE: Shush. Come here. I'm not interested in your soul.

Hand in hand they go towards the back of the stage and disappear behind the screen.

The stage is empty for a moment. SHE comes out from behind the screen, takes the packet of cigarettes and lighter from his shirt pocket, picks up the exercise book off the floor, opens it and reads for a moment.

HE: (*Behind the screen*) Did you find the cigarettes?

SHE: Yes.

HE: (*Behind the screen*) What're you doing? Why don't you come here?

SHE: (*Puts the exercise book inside the trunk and shuts it.*) Coming. (*Disappears behind the screen.*)

Silence. After a few moments there's a noise and the trapdoor opens once more. SHE appears, HE is behind her. They're both dressed exactly as they were at the start.

SHE: (*Waving at the space*) The attic. End of journey.

HE (*Puts his head through the trapdoor*) You sure this ladder's safe?

She: Yes, of course, don't be afraid.

HE's just climbed inside, takes hold of her from behind and kisses her on the neck.

SHE: That's strange.

HE: What is?

SHE: The lights are on. (*Disentangles from him.*) Don't be so clingy! (*Brief pause.*) I never leave them on.

HE: You slipped up. Nobody's perfect.

SHE: (*Goes to the back, looks behind the screen*) Nobody there.

HE: Who did you think would be there? Does anyone else have a key to the house?

SHE: No.

HE: So then? (*Goes to the foreground, sees the shirt and pants and picks them up.*) That is really strange.

SHE: What have you found?

HE: This shirt. It was here on the ground. And, look: it's identical to mine.

SHE: (*Comes over to check*) Yes, you're right.

HE: The pants as well.

SHE: (*Facetiously*) Not so sure about that.

HE: (*Puts clothing on armchair*) Want to see? (*Acts as if to unzip his flies.*)

SHE: No need. I'll believe you. (*Sees the Polaroid on the ground and picks it up.*) Look, I exhausted myself looking for this everywhere and it was here all the time.

HE: Does it work?

SHE: I think so.

HE (*A touch sourly*) Watch out, the devil loads these things.

SHE: (*Looking through the viewer*) Don't you like having your photo taken?

HE: I never have. Can't stand it. My face always comes out so.... That's all it is. (*Brief pause.*) It's a real drama whenever I have to renew my ID card. It's a bigger effort for me to go to the photographer's than to the dentist's.

SHE takes a photo of him.

HE: What are you doing? (*Chases her and she wriggles away.*) Give me that!

SHE: I don't want to!

HE: I told you to give it me! (*Catches her.*) Give it to me! (*Wrestling with her.*)

She: You're hurting me!

HE: Let go then, give it to me!

SHE: Take it then.

HE grabs the camera, walks away from her, puts the camera down in a corner, tears the photo up.

SHE: You hurt me. You wild beast!

HE: I told you I couldn't stand having my photo taken. (*He drops the bits on the floor, goes back over to her.*) Well, what did I do?

SHE: Get away. You hurt me.

HE: I'm sorry. If you hadn't held on so hard, it wouldn't have.

SHE: You're an animal! A wild beast!

HE: I've asked you to forgive me. I'm really sorry. I didn't mean to hurt you.

SHE: That would be all I needed!

HE: I just can't stand having my photo taken. I did tell you. It wasn't as if you didn't know. I can't stand it!

SHE: What about me? How am I supposed to put up with you? (*Pause. Walks towards the ladder.*) Let's go.

HE (*Catches her arm*) Where you going now?

SHE: I want out of this place.

HE: Don't be in such a rush, love. (*Holds her tight.*) Where did I hurt you?

SHE: (*She shows him the wrist*) Just here.

HE: (*Takes her hand gently, brings it to his lips and kisses the bruised part, lingers*) Hey, will you forgive me?

SHE: You're like a little kid.

HE: Will you forgive me? Say you'll forgive me.

SHE: Sometimes you scare me.

HE: You mustn't be scared of me. You know I love you.

SHE: (*Moves brusquely away from him*) Yes, you're always saying so. You always say so. (*Goes towards the big window and opens it. Daylight rushes in.*)

61

HE: What are you doing?

SHE: Ventilating this place. It smells shut up. (*Goes to the left corner and flicks a switch, the bulb on the right goes out.*) Put the other light out, please.

HE: How does it switch off?

SHE: Loosen the bulb.

HE: (*Burns his fingers trying*) Ouch! (*Picks up the pants and loosens the bulb with them over his hand.*) I tell you, they really are identical to mine. Isn't that very strange?

SHE: Strange, as in strange.... What do you expect me to say? They are an ordinary pair of pants. Give them to me. (*Picks them and shirt up from the armchair.*) I'll take them down to wash. God knows who left them here.

HE: You really want us to go?

SHE: I want to go now. You always spoil things. You've got a special knack.

HE: It's not that bad. Come here.

HE takes her arm, pulls her towards him, kisses her on the mouth. At first SHE resists, then yields and embraces him violently. Suddenly pulls away from him.

HE: What's the matter now? Are you crying? (*Pause.*) I don't understand you.

SHE: Let me be.

SHE goes to the window, looks outside. HE follows her and gently puts his arm round her shoulders.

HE: You did tell me you could see the sea from here, but you can't. That house blocks the view now.

SHE: Let me be.

HE: I'm sorry. What a state you're in! (*Walks through the attic, looks behind the screen, stops in front of the trunk and tries to open it. Can't.*) What's up with this trunk? Is it shut? Locked, I mean?

SHE: Yes. And the key went missing a long time ago. No big deal, there's nothing valuable inside.

HE: (*Struggles to open trunk*) I think if you could find something to act as a lever I could open it, the lock isn't very strong.

SHE: And why should you want to open it? Didn't I just say there's nothing of interest inside?

HE: The hinges have come away. I bet you can open it at the back. Look, no need even to force the lock. It even looks like someone else tried to open it this way. If I pull it out a bit... (*Pulls the trunk to the front of the stage.*)

SHE: (*Irritable*) For the last time can you let it be! I told you there's nothing in it!

HE: (*Surprised*) OK! Obviously I can't get a single thing right today! (*Crouches down again.*)

SHE: I told you not to touch it!

HE: (*Fishing for the trousers that had fallen behind the trunk.*) Hell, I'm not touching it! And look what I've found here. Some trousers! What do you bet they're identical to mine? (*Checks them out.*) Absolutely. Belt and all. A twin. It's like a bad joke. Please tell me who's playing what.

SHE: (*Takes the trousers*) Why ask me? What do you expect me to say? I've not a clue about these clothes.

HE: And you clearly expect me to believe that. (*Pause.*) Just as I've got to believe there's nothing important in the trunk. I believe you, I believe you, no need to pull that face... (*Returns to the trunk. Responds to her silent gesture.*) I'm not going to touch it! I couldn't care less what's inside! (*Pulls out some socks from behind the trunk.*) Look. (*Lifts them up triumphantly, like a trophy.*) All that's missing now are the shoes. Shoes exactly the same as mine obviously. Bet they're running around here. (*Looks around the floor, on all fours. Finds them.*) What did I tell you? We've got the lot now!

SHE: (*Violently grabs the clothing from his grasp*) Give me that!

HE: (*Surprised, protesting*) Hey, hey! Where you going?

SHE rolls clothing into a bundle, goes to the window and throws it out.

HE: Why did you do that, pray? (*Pause.*) Love, I think you've got a screw loose. (*Pause.*) Perhaps we should leave. (*Goes over to the ladder.*)

SHE: (*Looks out of window*) You go, if you want. I'd prefer to stay here by myself for a while.

HE: (*Stops*) So you want to stay here now? Understand you and I'd have you.

SHE: I feel very upset. I don't know what's got into me.

HE: That's no news to me.

SHE: (*Goes to the armchair and sits*) I'll rest for a while. I'll soon get over it. You wait downstairs if you like.

HE: Where shall I wait? In the bedroom? All showered and sweet-smelling?

SHE: (*Irritably*) Wait wherever you want! (*Pause.*) And if you don't want to wait, don't bother.

HE: Know what? I'll wait here. (*Walks though the attic, inspecting objects. Walks behind the screen. Comes back out, trailing a mattress. Closes the trapdoor, puts the mattress over it and lies down.*) Look what I've found. I can wait for you as long as is necessary and in total comfort. What's more, nobody can disturb us here. They couldn't open the trapdoor.

Silence.

HE: Hey! Didn't you say you wanted to rest? Come here then. You'll be much better.

SHE: I'm fine where I am, thank you very much.

Pause.

HE: Hey!

SHE: What do you want now?

HE: (*Gets up*) Give me a cigarette. I've none left.

SHE: No need to move, here.... (*Throws him the packet.*) And the lighter.... (*Throws him the lighter.*) I want you to stay where you are.

HE: We are prickly, aren't we? (*Sits down again, lights the cigarette.*) Here I was thinking we'd get close today.

Pause.

SHE: Me too.

HE: That you were bringing me here so we could fuck, in other words.

SHE: Shut up.

HE: Maybe I wasn't far out? You did say the other day you were fed up of the car and hotel rooms. Or didn't you?

SHE: Please for heaven's sake: shut up or go downstairs. I need to be quiet for a while. Just for a while. I don't think that's asking for too much. Some peace and quiet, for a while!

HE: It's only just been built, right?

SHE: What?

HE: The house. The house that blocks out the sea. It's been built recently?

SHE: It wasn't there, when I was a kid.

HE: I should be the one's who's angry, and not you.

SHE: I'm not angry.

HE: I'm delighted. You are not angry. But I should be.

SHE: And why should you be angry?

HE: Do you mind telling me why we've never come here before? It's a great bloody house, and you are the one moaning on about the car and hotel rooms. You've never mentioned this place. (*Pause.*) Tell me what you used it for? Who did you come here with?

SHE: For heaven's sake!

HE: No, I couldn't care a fuck. (*Puts his cigarette out, stamps on it violently.*) You can do whatever you want. You're a free woman. But don't then come telling me we're dirtying everything, that our relationship is becoming sordid.

SHE: For heaven's sake!

HE: Yes, sordid! That word sticks right here, doesn't it? Sordid! My lady thinks that our relationship is becoming sordid!

SHE: For heaven's sake, forget it. I'm just going through a bad patch, and you know that.

HE gets up from the mattress, goes over to the armchair and holds out a hand. SHE takes it and gets up. HE takes her by the shoulders and looks into her eyes.

HE: And you do know that I love you.

SHE: Yes...

HE: And that where love exists, there can be nothing sordid. (*Kisses her gently on the lips, moves away from her and to the window. Looks down.*) Bloody hell! That's a good drop! The house doesn't seem so high up from down there. Look, the bits of clothing you threw out landed on the garden table.

SHE: (*Walks over and looks out. Sticks her head out*) Guess what we did when I was a kid?

HE: When you could still see the sea?

SHE: It was a great view; the sunsets were beautiful. You know? There used to be pigeons up here. We used to play at throwing pigeon feathers out of the window. The one whose feathers landed on the garden table was the winner.

HE: Who used to play here? You and who else?

SHE: My cousins and I. You going to be jealous of my cousins as well?

HE: Cousins? What happened to these cousins of yours? Perhaps the clothes belonged to one of them.

SHE: Who knows where they've ended up. It's been years since I've seen them. I think the older one got married. (*Pause.*) So what anyway?

Silence.

HE: Got you! (*Grabs her from behind and holds her around the waist.*)

SHE: You animal! You frightened me!

HE steps back, keeps hold of her until they both fall on the mattress.

HE: Now I've got you where I wanted you.

SHE: Let go of me! Cheeky thing! I told you to let me be!

HE: 'You animal', 'cheeky thing' and, a moment ago, 'you wild beast' – you've got a nice way with nice words. (*Lets her go and sits at the other end of the mattress, holding his knees with his hands.*) Will you forgive me?

SHE: You're impossible.

HE: Will you forgive me?

SHE: (*Sighs, opens her arms*) Come here.

HE almost throws himself on top of her. They kiss passionately. HE tries to take her clothes off.

SHE: Wait. I don't want to get anything dirty. Or torn.

SHE stands, takes off her shoes with her feet while unbuttoning her blouse. HE, kneeling on the mattress, unzips her long skirt and struggles to undo a hook that offers resistance.

SHE: Don't be so impatient. Be careful.

HE undoes the hook, pulls her skirt down to the ground. SHE takes off her blouse, is now down to her underwear. SHE carefully folds her clothes and puts them on the trunk, then sees the Polaroid photo on the ground. Picks it up and looks at it, surprised.

SHE: Well, this is a find. Here, take a look.

HE (*Takes the photo and looks at it*) What kind of joke is this?

SHE: You asking me? I don't know. (*Pause.*) I thought you'd be able to tell me.

HE: Me? What do you expect me to say? (*Pause.*) It's not me, for starters.

SHE: For starters I reckon it's you all right.

HE: Nobody has ever taken that kind of photo of me!

SHE: Then you've got a twin brother.

HE: (*Looking again*) Naked? A photo stark naked?

SHE: Aren't you going to tear it up?

HE: What?

SHE: The photograph. Aren't you going to tear it up?

HE: It was taken here, that's clear enough... right here.

SHE: I just realized.

HE: And it's the first time I've been here...

SHE: Just what I was thinking...

HE: What you were just thinking? (*Pause.*) What's going through your head now?

SHE: I don't know. You tell me.

HE: I can tell you, can I? And what exactly can I tell you?

SHE: Up to you. I've been carrying the keys to this house in my purse for ages.

HE: What are you suggesting now? That I took them? That I came here...

SHE: You must know with whom.

HE: You're mad!

SHE: (*Excitedly*) Mad? And what about the photo? And the clothes? Explain the clothes?

HE: So, let's see.... (*Puts the photo on the mattress. Gets up.*) In other words, according to you I stole the keys from your purse. Then, through some mysterious intuition, I guessed they belonged to a house that happened to be in this village, on this road and at this number.... No, wait a minute, perhaps I didn't, perhaps I just decided to try all the locks in the country till I found they belonged here.... Well? (*Pause.*) When I'd done that, I rang a girl and told her to come here, and not to forget her camera, because I really wanted some photos of myself because, as everyone knows, I like people taking my photo, I'm delighted when they do! And what's more I wanted her to take me stark naked, because I hadn't a photo taken in my birthday suit since I was two. You know, the ones with your bum sticking up, perched on a cushion.... Wait, wait, I've not finished yet. My girlfriend turns up. And naturally you'll understand we didn't just take photos, we did other things. So far so

71

good? Then, in the grips of erotic frenzy, I not only left behind the photo of me stark naked, but went home in the nude, drove a hundred and fifty kilometres home in the nude, because I also left the clothes, my clothes here, right? Is that what you were thinking? Not far off, right? (*Grabs her by the shoulder and shakes her.*) Come on, out with it, is that what you were thinking?

SHE: No!

HE: So what were you thinking? Out with it!

SHE: Nothing at all! I don't get it at all! And shall I tell you something for nothing? I couldn't care less! I don't mind not getting it! Perhaps the guy in the photo isn't you, perhaps it's someone who looks like you. Perhaps it's just a bunch of coincidences. Coincidences I don't understand. And don't want to understand! All I do know is that I was really looking forward to coming here with you. That I'd waited a long time before suggesting we should come here. And now I couldn't care less! Get that? Couldn't care less?

Pause.

HE: It's all shit!

SHE: You know what all this is? A mistake. Yes, I made a mistake. So what? You and I were all right as we were. Making the most of your odd bits of spare time. The afternoon you'd ring home to say you had a meeting. Or in a hotel, the night you decided you had to travel because of your work. Not very many nights like that, all told. I remember every single one. Every hotel. Every room. Every bed.

HE: You didn't ever ask for anything else.

72

SHE: Right. (*Picks up her blouse and puts it on without buttoning it up.*)

HE: But we've only just got here. We've two days. We mustn't waste them.

SHE: We have already.

HE: (*Takes the photo, tears it down the middle and drops the two bits on the floor, between the window and the mattress*) Not yet. Let's erase all this.

SHE: What do you want us to erase?

HE: You're right. Nothing has really happened.

SHE: Yes, it has. You, as usual, didn't even notice.

HE: What then?

SHE: Forget it.

HE: I don't want to. I love you.

SHE: That word flows so easily from your lips! I love you, I love you, I love you.... I've never used that word with you. Have I? Have I ever? Have I ever told you I loved you?

HE: No! Never! I whistled and you came running! Like a bitch! But I have with you! And will again! I love you, I love you, I love you, I love you.... (*Embraces her violently. Kisses her against her wishes.*)

SHE: (*Struggles to disentangle herself, to no avail*) Let go, you're hurting me! You're revolting!

73

HE: I won't let you go! I won't let you go ever, right? Never again! (*Pulls her blouse violently.*) This has got to stop!

SHE: (*Still struggling, frightened*) Let me be! Fuck off! You're hurting me! I don't want to! I don't want to! You hear me?

HE: (*Ripping her blouse off, finally*) This has got to stop!

SHE: Has got to stop? (*Pause.*) It already has! Can't you see that?

HE: No! (*Pause.*) No way this has stopped! I want you. I desire you. I've never desired anything so much ever.

HE grabs her, SHE struggles. HE slaps and beats her until SHE falls on to the mattress.

HE: Come here! Come here!

HE stands over her. SHE is on the floor, crying.

SHE: Is this what you want? Is this what you desire? To rape me?

HE: Rape you? Me? (*Slowly, calmly, he pulls her legs apart, undoes his trousers, puts his foot on top of her.*)

SHE: No! Please! No!

HE: (*Calm*) Shut up! Don't shout! Don't say anything else! Be quiet! Quiet! (*Puts his hands on her neck and squeezes.*) Time's slipping through our fingers, can't you see? Slipping through our fingers... and we have to catch what we can, salvage what we can. However! We can't just let it escape. Time hurts. Always. When we don't have any, because we don't have any, when we do have some, because we talk too much. It's got to stop now! (*Lets go of her.*) I love you, you hear? (*Realizes SHE is inert.*) You hear me? Hey! (*Shakes her.*) Hey! (*Suddenly realizes she may be dead. Gets up from the mattress. Zips up. Doesn't know what to do. Stands and stares at her silently, for one long moment. Suddenly crouches down again, as if he'd noticed her moving.*) Hey! (*Realizes she is dead. Suddenly starts looking for the Polaroid camera, finds it. Goes back to the body. Crouches down. With difficulty, takes off her bra and knickers. Picks up the rest of her clothes that are scattered around. Bundles them all together and throws them out of the window. Takes the camera and photographs the body. Waits for the photo to come out. Takes it from the camera. Stands and stares at it until the image is formed. Bursts into tears. Looks for the two bits of the photo he tore up. Puts the two photos together. Looks at them. Continues to sob and shake.*)

Knocking. Someone tries to open the trapdoor from underneath. HE drops the photos, takes her body in his arms, doesn't know what to do. The knocking continues. HE hides her body behind the screen, goes back to the centre of the stage. The trap begins to open. HE jumps on the mattress and the trapdoor shuts beneath it. A female VOICE can be heard from under the trapdoor.

VOICE: I don't know what's wrong with it. I can't open it.

On hearing this, HE moves away from the mattress, to the left. Looks at the mattress. Nothing happens for a moment. Someone tries again and the trapdoor opens. The mattress slides until it leaves a space free. SHE appears, dressed as at the beginning. They both look at each other, disconcerted. She suddenly turns her head and looks around, and then, even more disconcerted, looks at him again. HE, unexpectedly, throws himself out of the window. Noise of him hitting the ground. She screams. She climbs into the attic, goes over to the window but doesn't dare put her head outside. Slowly, she slumps to the floor, where she stays curled up and shaking, whimpering like an injured animal. HE comes up through the trapdoor.

HE: What's the matter? What was the scream about? (*Pulls himself up quickly and goes over to her.*) What is it? What's happened?

SHE: (*Excitedly, stammering*) The window...

HE: What's wrong with the window? (*Goes over, puts his head out and looks down.*)

SHE: No!

HE: Don't worry, I'm being careful. (*Waves to someone, someone presumably in the garden.*) Hello! We'll be down right away.

SHE: What are you doing? Who are you speaking to?

HE: Who do you think? To Julià. She's getting the table ready for dinner. (*Turns round and looks at her.*) But what's wrong with you?

SHE: I don't know.

HE: You're shaking all over. (*Helps to her to get up. Hugs her warmly.*) Come on now, calm down. Everything's fine.

SHE: (*Still hugging him, moves her head away as much as she can to get him in focus*) Is that really you? Are you really here?

HE: What a thing to ask! Obviously it's me! Can't you see?

SHE: Yes, I can. (*Snuggles her head against his chest.*)

HE: Are you feeling better?

SHE nods.

HE: You sure?

SHE: (*Slowly separates from him, breathes deeply*) Yes. I'm better now.

HE: Now will you please tell me what was wrong? Why did you shout out? Where were all those questions leading?

SHE: (*Calmer*) The fact is I don't know. I really don't know what to say. (*Pause.*) I, I saw you... saw you here, next to the window...

HE: Now I see, and you were afraid I'd fall. But I told you before. The way you were shouting before I came up. That's precisely why I hurried up.

SHE: I know. I know you were coming behind. That's what I'm trying to tell you. I'm trying to tell you that when I opened the trapdoor I saw you by the window... and saw you take a jump... and heard the sound of your body hitting....

HE looks surprised.

SHE: It was awful! Before you jumped you gave me such a look... you seemed to hate me so much...

HE: It's those pills your doctor forces you to take. You've had a hallucination... you've been daydreaming. When we go down you can tell your brother-in-law all about it. Let's see what he makes of it.

77

SHE: But he specializes in entrails. What does he know about things of the mind?

HE: A doctor is a doctor. Let him give his opinion. And for the moment don't take any more pills! I didn't like them anyway. They're very potent.

SHE: But it was all so real...

HE: Come here.

SHE offers slight resistance.

HE: Don't be afraid.

SHE goes with him to the window. They both look down. Some light music can be heard in the distance – the latest pop – as if someone has a radio in the garden below. It continues playing to the end of the play. HE waves again.

HE: You see? It's all perfectly normal. Nothing's happened.

SHE: Nothing has happened. The psychiatrist never told me anything like this might happen.

HE: Well, he... come on then. Forget about it. Shall we go down?

SHE: Not yet. You know I wanted to show you something.

HE: You did say those exercise books of yours we brought here that day. I've not forgotten. But we can leave it for another time, if you'd rather.

SHE: No, I'm fine now.

HE: You sure?

SHE: Really. Come here. (*Goes to the trunk and opens it easily. Taken aback and disappointed*) Oh no!

HE: Aren't they there?

SHE: There are only toys and old clothes.

HE: But we left everything in here. We filled four or five cardboard boxes, loaded them in the car and brought them here.

SHE: I'm surprised you have such a clear memory.

HE: Of course I do. I was the one who had to cart everything up here! And I swear, paper weighs heavy!

SHE: I helped.

HE: Yes. You opened doors and pointed the way, but I was the one who sweated. I remember it as if it were yesterday.

SHE: It must be six years ago.

HE: Seven. Next month will make seven. (*Kisses her.*) So they're not here?

SHE: I just said. Toys and old clothes. In very neatly folded piles, that's for sure. And with little bags of lavender here and there. (*Takes one out and sniffs.*)

HE: It's Julià's hallmark. The smart and tidy hippy that is your big sister.

79

SHE: If she could hear you...

HE: Yes, she'd be furious. She used to tell us about her little run-ins in Formentera and Menorca, and I'd say, 'Come on. You've never been a proper hippy... who's ever seen a smart, tidy hippy....' But now, I bet she doesn't even remember. Look at her now, the doctor's wife, in her trouser suits and necklaces.... The smart, tidy hippy.

SHE: Obviously, this is her doing. From the time when she emptied the house in Menorca and came to live here.

HE: She must have thrown them away. (*Starts poking in the trunk.*)

SHE: Julià? You don't know her. She never throws anything away.

HE: (*Looks up as if he's heard something*) Shush.

SHE: What?

HE: I heard a car.

SHE: (*Runs to the window. Eagerly*) Marta? Already?

The sound of a car engine. A dog barking. The car stops. The car horn hoots. The dog barks more loudly.

HE: Always making a din. (*Takes a doll from the trunk. Its head has come apart from its body. Tries to put it back.*)

SHE: Be nice to her, won't you?

HE: Have you ever known me not be?

80

SHE: You know what I mean. Last year you wouldn't leave her alone. You criticized everything. Her hairdo, make-up, the clothes she wore....

The sound of a car-door shutting.

SHE: (*Shouts through the window*) Marta! We're here!

This pause and subsequent ones correspond to what Marta's saying from the garden and which we can't hear.

SHE: We'll be down in a second. I was looking for something.

Pause.

SHE: He's up here with me.

Pause.

SHE: Don't be silly!

Pause.

SHE: You know I like him!

Pause.

SHE: (*To him*) Come here, this mad woman says she wants to see if you're still so handsome.

HE goes over to the window, waves the headless doll.

SHE: (*To Marta*) What was that?

Pause.

SHE: I don't want to hear any more of that! (*Turns to him and kisses him on the lips. To HE*) I always feel happy when I see Marta. We see each other so rarely.

HE: Ladies and gentlemen, Chekov is all ready to go.

SHE: What do you mean now?

HE: That the three sisters are here.

SHE: Yes. 'The Three Sisters'.... You know what? I still know Irina's part by heart. Listen...

HE: I'd keep quiet about it.

SHE: Do you think I'm such a bad actress? Listen: 'The day will come when men will find out the reason for all of that, for so much suffering. Then there'll be no mystery. In the meantime, we must get on with life. Must work and work. I'll leave tomorrow by myself. What does any of this matter....'

HE: That's from the end, isn't it?

SHE: Yes.

HE: I don't know why I decided to bring up 'The Three Sisters'. (*Throws the doll inside the trunk.*) I'm sorry. I'm stupid. After playing Irina you had your first attack of depression.

SHE: Irina wasn't to blame.... Poor Irina. It was six months before I found any work. That was the cause.

HE: But I didn't have to speak about the theatre now. It's too hurtful for you.

SHE: Do you still think so? I'm really not so sure. More than once it's helped me find the words I needed to say things I wouldn't otherwise have been able to express.... Now I think about it, Irina was a kind of premonition.

HE: Forget it.

SHE: 'Where has everything gone? Where has everything departed? My God, my God! I've forgotten everything! My head is in such a mess. I can't remember how you say road in Italian or ceiling. I am forgetting everything, every day I forgot more and more. And life ebbs and ebbs and will never come back, never! And we will never go to Moscow! I see that clearly enough. Never!'

HE: Don't torture yourself anymore. Just forget it. They are only words for the stage, words that have been stolen. Like old clothes, worn by someone else.... They're not your words, or your clothes.

SHE: (*As if she had not heard*) True enough, Julià and Andreu went there not long ago, to some sort of congress...

HE: Where?

She: To Moscow.... (*Ponders.*) Is it Moscow or Moscouw?

HE: What are you on about?

SHE: Did you see the long skirt Marta was wearing?

HE: What?

SHE: I saw the way you were looking at her.

HE: Well, she is good-looking.

SHE: You men. You've got one-track minds.

HE: What about you women? Do you think I couldn't hear what your sister was saying to you? 'It probably is a good idea. Before dinner, this is the best aperitif.'

HE embraces her, and they kiss and linger. SHE separates from him.

SHE: (*Playful, as if suddenly having a bright idea*) I've got it! It's so obvious!

HE: So very obvious! The aperitif's at an end...

SHE: I think I know where the exercise books are. You'll see.

SHE goes to the back of the stage and disappears behind the screen. Silence. Only the music coming from the garden can be heard. HE stays near the window, sees something on the floor and picks it up. It's the two Polaroid photos, one intact and the other torn down the middle. HE looks at them. Smiles. Puts them in his shirt pocket.

HE: I've found something!

SHE: (*Behind the screen*) What did you say?

HE: (*Louder*) I said I've found something!

SHE: I haven't yet. What have you found?

HE: I'm not telling you. It's a surprise.

SHE: You can hardly see anything back here. It's very dark.... But wait, I reckon I've got them now. (*Emerges with a bundle of exercise books tied with string.*) It must be one of these. What did you say you've found?

HE (*Takes out the photos and shows them to her*) Look.

SHE: (*Puts the bundle of books on the floor, takes the photos and looks at them*) How funny! You took this one on the sly, when I was asleep, you traitor, you bastard.

HE: You were so pretty I couldn't resist the temptation.

SHE: I look as if I was dead.

HE: Don't say such things!

SHE: On the other hand, I took one of you when you were all alive and perky. Why did you tear it in half?

HE: I didn't. It was like that.

SHE: A pity. Perhaps with a bit of Sellotape.... You know I thought we had these photos at home.

HE: So did I.

SHE: If they were ordinary photos you might think they were copies. But Polaroids...

HE: Perhaps we did leave them here, after all.

SHE: Maybe.... They look as if they were taken a moment

ago. They look strange, don't they?

HE: Yes, But they're getting on in years. Give them to me and I'll put them away. You've not got any pockets. (*Takes them and puts them back in his shirt pocket.*)

SHE: We took them more than six years ago.

HE: Next month, it will be seven. How often do I have to tell you?

SHE: I can hardly believe we're still together.... You know I am a very lucky woman?

HE: And I'm a very fortunate man.

SHE: Do you really mean that?

HE: Don't you believe me?

SHE: Yes.... I believe you. (*Crouches, undoes the string round the bundle.*) The sun will soon set and I must first find that exercise book. Not this one, or that one. (*She leafs through*) Here it is. Listen: 'It's very bad to tell lies, and that's why I never tell any. My big sister tells lots of lies. My younger sister doesn't, because she doesn't know how to talk yet.'

HE: Is that what you wanted to read to me? Is that what we came up here for?

SHE: It's a composition from when I was at school.

HE: I can see that, How old were you?

SHE: Ten, I expect. Julià was eighteen and Marta was two.

HE: It's odd. Three girls. And such gaps between you.

SHE: Our parents thought everything through. They wanted to do things properly. (*Pause.*) Wait, I've not finished yet. 'Mother says that if you tell lies your teeth will fall out. But Julià's teeth aren't falling out. I think that must be a lie, because grown-ups sometimes tell them too. (*Puts down the book and carries on, as if still reading. The light is fading and turning red.*) Lies are like cherries, you eat one after another and can't stop. And in the end it's as if it wasn't you, as if another person has invaded your body, and you were wearing a skin that wasn't yours.'

HE: You didn't write that when you were ten.

SHE: No.

Pause.

HE: Tell me the truth. Why have we come here? What do you want to know?

SHE: How long have you been seeing Marta?

HE: A year.

SHE: It was after that dinner last year, right? When you drove her home because her car had broken down?

HE: Yes.

SHE: And you weren't going to say a word to me?

HE: No.

87

SHE: Why not?

HE: At the start because I thought it was a passing affair that would soon be over, and I didn't want to hurt you.

SHE: And then.

HE: Then, I'm not sure. I was frightened. I was frightened for your sake. You'd been ill. You still weren't right. You still aren't.

SHE: And we'd all have had dinner together today and all sat smiling round the table. As if nothing had happened. Right?

HE: That's what I was hoping.

Pause.

SHE: I love you. I know this isn't what I should be saying now. But it's what's come into my head. I love you.

HE: I know.

SHE: Knowing isn't enough.

HE: I don't know what came over me…. I don't know what happened.

SHE: Yes, you do. Time goes by. That's what's happened. (*She gets up.*) Say to me. 'Take your blouse off'.

HE: Why?

SHE: Say it. Don't ask me any more stupid questions.

HE: Take your blouse off.

SHE: (*Unbuttons and takes it off*) Now say, 'Take your skirt off'.

HE: Listen. None of this makes any sense.

SHE: Say it!

HE: (*Pauses*) Take your skirt off.

SHE: (*Takes off her skirt*) Go on. All by yourself. You don't need me to dictate to you, do you?

HE: Take your bra off.

SHE: (*Takes off her bra.*) Do you still like looking at me?

HE: Do I still? I wouldn't know what to do without you.

SHE: But you don't know what to with me either, do you? (*Pause.*) Knickers?

HE: Please.

SHE: (*Takes off her knickers, stands naked in front of him. Turns and looks through the window*) Look, the sun's setting over the water. The sea seems like a sheet of copper.

HE: The sea.... I... I don't know what to say. I don't know what to say.

SHE: Don't say anything.

HE: They're waiting for us downstairs.

SHE: Let them wait. Come here.

SHE holds a hand out to him. HE takes it. They sit on the mattress.

SHE: Know what? The body can't lie.

Pause. HE looks at her for a long time.

HE: No. No, it can't.

HE kisses her on the forehead. Gets up, goes over to the trapdoor, goes down and disappears. SHE is left alone, naked, sitting in front of the last rays of the sun that tinge her red. SHE gets up, takes the Polaroid and takes a photo of the sunset. She waits for the photo to take shape. Night falls. The sound of a car starting up, a dog barking. Then, just the radio.

The Sale

Lluïsa Cunillé

First performed at the Grec 97 Festival
Teatre Adrià Gual, Barcelona
17 July 1997

Cast:

Glòria	–	Marta Millà
Marta	–	Àurea Màrquez
Eduard	–	Ramon Vila

Creative Team:

Director	–	Yvette Vigatà
Set Design	–	Tobia Escorlino
Lighting	–	Nuccio Marino
Sound	–	Michel Maldonado

Translated into English by Laura McGloughlin

ACT ONE

An empty room in an old apartment. A distant dripping sound can be heard from time to time. MARTA looks out of the window and GLÒRIA looks at MARTA. A long pause.

GLÒRIA: There's nobody downstairs, and there's only an old couple living upstairs.

Pause.

MARTA: What used to be here?

GLÒRIA: A dining room... well, a dining area.

MARTA: Is it possible to put a phone in here?

GLÒRIA: Yes, and central heating as well.

MARTA: Where I live now isn't half the size of this but then I don't pay much rent.

Pause.

GLÒRIA: The truth is I'm in a bit of a rush...

MARTA: What?

GLÒRIA: To sell the flat.

MARTA: Oh.

GLÒRIA: Would you like me to turn on the lights?

MARTA: No, there's no need.

Pause.

GLÒRIA: What do you think? Don't you like it?

MARTA: Yes... yes.

GLÒRIA: You can open the window if you like.

MARTA: No, it's all right.

Pause.

GLÒRIA: Are you feeling alright?

MARTA: Yes.

GLÒRIA: Really?

MARTA: Yes... fine. No... not really.

GLÒRIA: What's the matter?

MARTA: I'm a little tired.

GLÒRIA: I'm sorry there's no chair.

MARTA begins to cry.

MARTA: I'm sorry.

GLÒRIA: Can I do anything?

MARTA: No, I'm sorry.

GLÒRIA goes out of the room and, after a few moments, returns with an empty wooden box.

GLÒRIA: Have a seat... sit down.

MARTA: No... it's OK.

GLÒRIA: Have a seat.

MARTA: (*Does not sit, continues to cry*) Don't think... I really like it, the flat.

GLÒRIA: Really?

MARTA (*Tries to smile*) Yes, but it's very expensive.

GLÒRIA: It's also very big.

MARTA: Yes it is.... And why are you selling it?

GLÒRIA: I've found work abroad.

MARTA: Abroad?

GLÒRIA: Yes.

MARTA: And you won't be coming back?

GLÒRIA: I don't know.

MARTA: No... I mean about the flat, if you sell it.

GLÒRIA: I need the money.

MARTA: Yes, of course.

Pause.

GLÒRIA: You don't need to tell me anything right now.

MARTA: But you are in a rush, aren't you?

GLÒRIA: Yes, but I can wait a few days.

MARTA: And are you going very far away to work?

GLÒRIA: Geneva.

MARTA: It's quite far.

GLÒRIA: I'm going to be an interpreter for the United Nations.

MARTA: Really?

GLÒRIA: Yes.

MARTA: I work in radio, I'm a producer. Well, I do a little of everything....

GLÒRIA: I never listen to the radio, I don't have much time now.

MARTA: Well, actually most people who listen to the radio do it while they're doing other things.

GLÒRIA: Yes, that's true. (*Pause.*) Are you feeling better?

MARTA: Yes... yes. Excuse me, but it's just that things haven't been good lately.

GLÒRIA: It's fine.

MARTA: Are you well? I mean are you looking forward to going to Geneva? That's what counts.

GLÒRIA: Well, until I get to Geneva I won't know for sure if I will like it or not.

MARTA: You've never been there?

GLÒRIA: Only a couple of times.

MARTA: And you're going alone? I beg your pardon, I ask too many questions. (*Pause.*) You won't laugh at me if I tell you something?

GLÒRIA: What?

MARTA: No, first you have to promise me you won't laugh.

GLÒRIA: I won't laugh.

MARTA: It's just that I've broken something.

GLÒRIA: What?

MARTA: The knob of the toilet door – it came off in my hand when I went to pull it.

GLÒRIA: No, it was already like that.

MARTA: Oh, it was already broken.

GLÒRIA: Yes, it has been for a while.

MARTA: (*Takes the knob from her bag.*) I tried to fix it on again but I couldn't.

GLÒRIA: (*Takes the knob*) Yes, it's quite difficult.

MARTA: I don't know why I didn't say it to you before.

GLÒRIA: It's fine. There's also a tap that drips, can you hear it? They should be coming to fix it now, any minute.

Pause.

MARTA: Has anyone ever interviewed you?

GLÒRIA: Me?

MARTA: Yes, on the radio.

GLÒRIA: No, never. Why?

MARTA: Right now I'm in charge of an interviews programme, we interview people that... well, people who do work that's a little bit specialised. Have you worked for the United Nations for a long time?

GLÒRIA: No, actually I'm only just starting now.

MARTA: Would you like it if we were to do an interview with you before you go?

GLÒRIA: Well, it's just that I don't have too much time now with all...

MARTA: Don't you like interviews?

GLÒRIA: No, it's not that... but I still have to sort out a lot of things before I go away. And since I haven't even started work yet...

MARTA: You would only have to talk about yourself.

GLÒRIA: Yeah, but it's just...

MARTA: You seem like a very interesting person.

GLÒRIA: Do I?

MARTA: Yes.

GLÒRIA: Being an interpreter isn't all that interesting.

MARTA: No, I'm talking about you. I have a good eye for people.

GLÒRIA: It's just that now I haven't time, really...

MARTA: So you don't want to do the interview?

GLÒRIA: Anyway, I wouldn't know what to say.

MARTA: Fine, no problem, no problem. (*Pause.*) My God, I don't know why I always want to cry. I don't know what comes over me. (*Pause.*) You know, I would like to be like you... to have your serenity....

GLÒRIA: My serenity?

MARTA: Recently I've been crying for no reason, over any old thing.

GLÒRIA: Lately I cry too.

MARTA: Pardon?

GLÒRIA: I said that I cry too.

MARTA: And what makes you cry?

GLÒRIA: I don't know, leaving my flat for example.

MARTA: You've cried for the flat?

GLÒRIA: Does that seem stupid to you?

MARTA: No, of course not. Sometimes I am afraid of myself, I frighten myself. What nonsense, eh?

Pause.

GLÒRIA: It makes me a little afraid, going to Geneva. I don't even know how to ice skate. It's just that beside Geneva there is a lake where you can see that everyone goes to ice skate after work. Anyway, I don't think I will have much time to do anything... and especially now with how things are.

MARTA: What things?

GLÒRIA: At the United Nations. They've reduced their staff a lot, mostly in Europe.

MARTA: I didn't know that.

GLÒRIA: Yes, I've clearly been very lucky. (*Pause.*) The first thing I'll do when I arrive in Geneva is buy myself a car, you can't go anywhere with the one I have now, it's a deathtrap. (*Pause.*) At the beginning I wanted to go to New York but it wasn't possible.

MARTA: Listen, why don't you let me do an interview with you now?

GLÒRIA: Now?

MARTA: Yes, here. (*Searches her bag.*)Where is it.... (*Pulls out a recording device.*) I always carry it on me for work. I record ideas... things that come to me so I won't forget them.

MARTA turns on the recording device and her voice is heard.

MARTHA'S VOICE: 'It's going very slowly. My God, what a face I'm making. Right... let's see... it would be... (*Pause.*) No, it's not working.'

MARTA: (*Turns off the recording device*) I recorded that while I was coming up in the lift – the one here. I'm not used to doing interviews, but if you don't have time to come to the studio.... What do you say?

GLÒRIA: I don't know. It's just that...

MARTA: You would only have to say what you were saying before.

GLÒRIA: What?

MARTA: About ice skating and the thing about the car....

GLÒRIA: You want me to talk about needing to buy a car?

101

MARTA: Yes, everything you told me.

GLÒRIA: I don't know. Also I don't know if I can explain the thing about the United Nations... that they're reducing their staff.

MARTA: It's a secret?

GLÒRIA: No... I don't know. But I don't know if I can say it. No, look, it's better if...

MARTA: Then we won't talk about the United Nations. We'll just talk about you. (*Presses buttons on the recording device while she is talking.*) Start with your name, your profession, a little about what you've done up to now, work, education... and all that.

GLÒRIA: But aren't you going to ask me any questions?

MARTA: First tell me all that and afterwards I'll ask you questions.

GLÒRIA: Is it already recording?

MARTA: (*The recording device in her hand*) You know... I'm thinking that I could interview you when you have settled in Geneva, two or three months from now. That way you could talk a little about the work you do there as well. How does that sound?

GLÒRIA: I don't know.

MARTA: Yes, that seems better to me. Besides, an interview from Geneva could be really good. (*She puts the recording device in her bag.*) You're not angry, are you?

GLÒRIA: No, why would I be angry...

MARTA: Yes, you are angry, it's obvious.

GLÒRIA: No, I'm not angry.

MARTA: Listen, we'll do the interview... come on. (*Looks for the recording device in her bag.*)

GLÒRIA: No, not now.

MARTA: Yes, come on.

GLÒRIA: No, we're not doing any interview now.

MARTA: (*Pulls out the recording device.*) Yes, come on.

GLÒRIA: I told you no.

Pause.

MARTA: I'm sorry... really... (*She leaves the recording device on the wooden box.*) I always want to do things right and everything comes out backwards... I ruin everything... I'm sorry... I'm sorry...

GLÒRIA: It's fine... it doesn't matter... (*GLÒRIA grabs the recording device from the top of the box.*) Here...

MARTA doesn't take the recording device. GLÒRIA pushes a button and then Marta's voice can be heard. "Yes... let's see... yeah... it would be based on people talking about whatever they want... they phone in and talk about whatever they feel like... nothing other than people talking... no music... no interruptions or anything... one call after another, that's it... end of story. (*Pause.*) This fear again... but fear of what? I'm going mad... completely mad... no... I'm fine! Oh my God... I'm fine!" (*The recording ends. GLÒRIA turns off the recorder. Pause.*)

MARTA: (*Grabbing the recording device*) Don't think... I never listen to it afterwards... it's been a while since I had a worthwhile idea... one that might be useful for work after.... I recorded all that while I was coming up in the lift... As it was going so slowly...

GLÒRIA: I never look at myself in lift mirrors.

MARTA: Are you scared of going mad too?

GLÒRIA: No, not of going mad, no.

MARTA: Then what are you scared of?

GLÒRIA: Now?

MARTA: Yes.... Don't be scared of anything...

GLÒRIA: Maybe of having to stay here...

MARTA: What... here?

GLÒRIA: I have to wait here until they come to fix the tap...

MARTA: Who?

GLÒRIA: I don't know... I don't know them. Anyway, I suppose they're not late yet.

Pause.

MARTA: I can wait until they come...

GLÒRIA: No, there's no need.

MARTA: They must be coming now, right?

GLÒRIA: It's just that you can't even sit down...

MARTA: It's alright.

GLÒRIA: (*Referring to the box*) Sit here if you'd like.

MARTA: No... sit down if you're tired...

GLÒRIA: No, sit down, really...

Pause.

MARTA: Listen... listen... how long can you wait to know about the flat?

GLÒRIA: I don't know...

MARTA: I'll let you know soon... within the next two days.

GLÒRIA: Alright.

MARTA: Because renting it...

GLÒRIA: What?

MARTA: Would it be possible that you would rent it instead of selling it?

GLÒRIA: Would it suit you better to rent it?

MARTA: Well... the truth is yes, it would.

GLÒRIA: It's not possible...

MARTA: Oh...

GLÒRIA: If I go and leave the flat without selling it... well... I think that from the beginning I did tell you that...

MARTA: Yes... you did tell me... I know. What's more, you also told me before that you needed the money... I thought I'd ask just in case.... When do you go?

GLÒRIA: To Geneva? In less than a month...

MARTA: Not long now... I think now it would really suit me to go to a place like Geneva. I've never been there but I can imagine it. What languages do you speak?

GLÒRIA: English.

MARTA: Me too... I could go there in your place. Obviously then you'd have to stay here in mine...

GLÒRIA: As a presenter?

MARTA: No... I'm a producer...

GLÒRIA: Oh, I thought you said you were...

MARTA: No, I work as a producer.

GLÒRIA: I understood you were a presenter... and seeing how you were going to interview me...

MARTA: It's alright... I do a little of everything anyway... if sometime you want to be a presenter I can test you... you have a really good voice... and if you know languages too...

GLÒRIA: I only know English...

MARTA: I can test you whenever you want... whenever suits you... (*She touches the light switch.*)

GLÒRIA: There's no current, it has to be turned on downstairs... If you want I'll put it on, it'll only take a moment...

MARTA: No, there's no need... really. (*Pause.*) You said no one lives upstairs, right?

GLÒRIA: No, there's an old couple, but they're never there.

MARTA: Is the flat theirs?

GLÒRIA: Yes, it's theirs. It's downstairs that's empty, but they're all offices.

Pause.

MARTA: I always have someone or other at home... relatives or friends... I live alone but really I'm never alone... if I were alone then I really would go mad. So I don't know how you do it... it would kill me! Not you? My God... I don't know why I'm talking about all this, now. Anyway... I never think about it... I don't spend all day thinking about this.... I'd like to have your serenity.

GLÒRIA: I think you're mistaken.

MARTA: No... I mean it. I have a good eye for people...

GLÒRIA: Well, this time you're wrong because I'm not serene at all... I'm going to Geneva and I don't really know why... I have to buy myself a car and again I don't know why... I have lived I don't know how many years in this flat and now that I'm going I don't know how I've borne so much time here... I've always done everything that really I don't want to do... so you see...

Pause.

MARTA: What is it you really wanted to do? Go to New York?

GLÒRIA: You haven't understood at all.

MARTA: No... tell me...

GLÒRIA: Leave it...

MARTA: Do you want to stay here?

Pause.

GLÒRIA: Right now I'd like to be anything other than myself... even this doorknob before being me. I'm tired of myself, understand? Completely tired. Listen... you're not recording all this, are you?

MARTA: What... of course not. I have the recorder in my bag... what do you take me... (*Takes the recording device from the bag.*) Here... listen if you want... here...

GLÒRIA: Look... it doesn't matter... record whatever you feel like recording...

MARTA: Honestly, I haven't recorded anything... you don't believe me? Look...

MARTA presses a button on the recording device, there are a few moments of silence and afterwards Marta's voice can be heard. "Let's see... tomorrow morning beginning from..."

MARTA: (*Turns off the recording device.*) That was mine... I recorded it a few days ago, I think... another of my ideas that came to nothing afterwards... (*She puts the recorder in her bag.*)

GLÒRIA: The one from before seems like a good idea to me...

MARTA: What?

GLÒRIA: The one where people phone in and talk about whatever they want... it's a very good idea...

MARTA starts laughing.

GLÒRIA: I mean it, it's a good idea...

MARTA: Yes, I know... but there's already a programme like that...

GLÒRIA: Really?

MARTA: (*Laughing more and more*) Yes...

GLÒRIA: I didn't know...

MARTA: Of course not, if you never listen to the radio...

GLÒRIA also starts to laugh. Pause.

GLÒRIA: Listen... if you can't wait any longer... there's no need for you to stay...

MARTA: (*Still laughing*) Do you want me to go?

GLÒRIA: No... but I'm making you wait all this time...

Pause.

MARTA: You could phone them to see if they're coming... I mean to fix the tap...

GLÒRIA: There's no phone here. Besides...

MARTA: What?

GLÒRIA: Besides... I don't have the number here...

They laugh even harder. Eventually, they stop.

MARTA: It's been a long time since I laughed like that...

GLÒRIA: Me too...

GLÒRIA: Now I'm not happy here...

MARTA: Yes, me too.... (*Pause.*) What am I saying? (*She is moving her lips soundlessly.*)

GLÒRIA: I don't understand you...

MARTA: No, look... what am I saying? (*She moves her lips again.*)

GLÒRIA: I don't know...

MARTA: Don't you know how to read lips?

GLÒRIA: No...

MARTA: I thought you would know... for work...

GLÒRIA: Do you know how?

MARTA: A bit... I learned it at the station...

GLÒRIA: What am I saying? (*She moves her lips.*)

MARTA: Say it again. (*Pause.*) I don't know. (*Pause.*) I don't know how to escape.

GLÒRIA: No... I don't know how to ice-skate.

MARTA: I almost got it right...

GLÒRIA: It was very easy.

MARTA: OK... now me. What am I saying? (*She moves her lips.*)

GLÒRIA: I don't know.

MARTA starts moving her lips again.

GLÒRIA: I don't know what you're saying.

MARTA stops.

GLÒRIA: What did you say?

MARTA: No... nothing... Besides it was too long. Listen... look... if you don't find anyone to buy the flat from you, I could rent it from you... only if you don't find someone, of course...

GLÒRIA: You don't want to buy it?

MARTA: Actually I think I can't.

GLÒRIA: Oh...

MARTA: But if you did rent it, how much would you ask for it? Just to give me an idea, even though you're not renting it...

GLÒRIA: I don't know...

MARTA: Approximately...

GLÒRIA: The truth is I don't know... I haven't thought about it...

MARTA: Of course not, if you want to sell it.

GLÒRIA: Really I don't know now...

MARTA: If you rented it you could always come back...

GLÒRIA: What?

MARTA: Later on... you could come back...

GLÒRIA: No, I could never come back to live here.

MARTA: No, of course not.

Pause.

GLÒRIA: You could try upstairs to see if they will rent it to you...

MARTA: The flat upstairs?

GLÒRIA: Yes...

MARTA: Have they told you they want to rent it?

GLÒRIA: No... but you could ask just in case... since they're never there.

MARTA: I'll ask, thank you.

GLÒRIA: I could give you the phone number, if you want...

MARTA: Yes, but if they're never there...

GLÒRIA: No, not the one here, another...

MARTA: Oh, very good. (*She searches her bag.*) Have you known them for a long time?

GLÒRIA: They're my parents.

MARTA: Ah...

GLÒRIA: Generally I don't tell the people who come to see the flat that the flat above belongs to my parents...

MARTA: Yes, I understand.

GLÒRIA: Besides, I don't know if they'll want to rent it to you...

MARTA: Is the flat the same as this one?

GLÒRIA: What... yes, the same. (*Pause.*) It's most likely they won't want to rent it to you...

MARTA: Oh... might as well try...

GLÒRIA: They come here from time to time.

MARTA: What's the number? (*She has a pen and a diary in her hand.*)

GLÒRIA: Look... maybe it's better if I call and ask them about it myself...

MARTA: What do you mean?

GLÒRIA: Yes, because they'll ask you who gave you their number anyway... it's better if I call.

MARTA: Afterwards, you'll let me know, won't you?

GLÒRIA: Yes, when I've spoken to them I'll call you.

MARTA: You have my number, don't you?

GLÒRIA: But you needn't say it to anybody... about my parents, that they're never there...

MARTA: No, I won't say anything.

GLÒRIA: Besides... I don't know if they'll rent it to you, I already told you.... (*Pause.*) Are you alright? Listen, you mustn't cry, OK?

MARTA: No, it's not that... really, I'm not crying about the flat. There... it's over... I won't cry anymore, really... that's it.

Pause.

GLÒRIA: And when are you coming to Geneva to interview me?

MARTA: To Geneva? No... well, actually we'll do the interview over the phone... didn't I tell you? No... I didn't tell you...

GLÒRIA: No... but I should have guessed anyway... it's obvious...

MARTA: I'm sorry... I thought I...

GLÒRIA: No... but if I'd thought about it...

MARTA: If you want we could interview you when you come back... in the holidays...

GLÒRIA: Which holidays?

MARTA: The summer holidays... or before, whenever it suits you... I'm sorry... I should have told you at the beginning... I'm sorry... I ruin everything... I always ruin everything...

The doorbell rings. GLÒRIA goes to the door of the room. Before going out, she stops, approaches MARTA and gives her a kiss.

MARTA: What's going on?

GLÒRIA: Nothing. (*She goes to the door and leaves.*)

MARTA: (*Louder*) You feel sorry for me, don't you? Eh? Eh? (*Almost to herself*) I'll never cry again... never again...

Blackout.

A dripping sound can be heard.

ACT TWO

The same empty room. EDUARD and MARTA are the only people there. Pause.

EDUARD: Don't you feel she's taking a long time?

MARTA: What? Pardon?

EDUARD: No... nothing. Listen... Marta, isn't it?

MARTA: Yes... Marta.

EDUARD: It seems to me that we're having our legs pulled, you understand me...

MARTA: What do you mean?

EDUARD: That the flat isn't hers... that... what's she called...

MARTA: Glòria.

116

EDUARD: She took I don't know how much time to turn on the lights, before you arrived. And now the water...

MARTA: Yes, she's taking a while.

EDUARD: Look, we should come to an agreement before she comes back. You like the flat, right?

MARTA: Yes...

EDUARD: Me too.

MARTA: Yes.

EDUARD: No... but listen, we could arrange it between ourselves...

MARTA: Arrange it... how?

EDUARD: We have to talk...

MARTA: She'll be back any moment now...

EDUARD: No... afterwards... now we have to act as if nothing...

MARTA: But...

EDUARD: As if we haven't talked about anything...

MARTA: I just stayed to say something...

EDUARD: Now?

MARTA: Yes... well... today...

EDUARD: Ah, well then...

MARTA: No... but we can talk before...

EDUARD: How long have you known her?

MARTA: Glòria?

EDUARD: Yes.

MARTA: We spoke here a week ago...

EDUARD: So you've seen the flat before...

MARTA: Yes... you haven't?

EDUARD: She's in a real hurry to get rid of the flat, don't you think?

MARTA: She has to go away...

EDUARD: Where?

MARTA: Travelling... abroad.

EDUARD: She told you that she had to go abroad?

MARTA: Yes, didn't she tell you?

EDUARD: No, I only met her today. Listen... is something the matter?

MARTA: Why?

EDUARD: No... no reason at all...

Pause.

MARTA: She's not coming...

EDUARD: There's no phone here, is there?

MARTA: No...

EDUARD: It's alright... I'll call afterwards.... Are you in a hurry? No... I mean about meeting afterwards.... We can have a drink and talk...

MARTA: Yes... we can meet...

EDUARD looks at the door. Pause.

EDUARD: I thought I heard her...

MARTA: The elevator only comes up.

EDUARD: What?

MARTA: Maybe she's taking a while because she had to go down on foot...

EDUARD: She... Glòria told me that you work on the radio...

MARTA: She told you I worked on the radio?

EDUARD: Yes, and because of that you'd certainly be late.... Don't you work on the radio?

MARTA: Yes.

119

EDUARD: I'm a master. My colleagues like to say that they're teachers. But I like master better. In the end it must be said I'm not one thing or the other...

MARTA: And what's the difference?

EDUARD: I don't know, but there must be a difference.... Listen... I've been looking... we could make a wall here... and each of us would take a part, as it's fairly big... of course we needn't say anything to Glòria, because she'd want to do it and raise the price of the flat on us...

MARTA: (*At the centre of the room*) Is this halfway?

EDUARD: Well... there's an extra room on this side but we could sort that out... as this side has no kitchen, whoever takes it will have an extra room to make a new kitchen... no, but listen... what if we talk about it afterwards, and meanwhile you mull it over.... You live alone, don't you? No... Glòria told me... look... it seems to me she went out on purpose... it's very difficult to sell a flat this big and in cash... but listen... we must seem as if we haven't agreed on it... well anyway, we still have to talk.... (*Pause. He looks at the wooden box.*) Don't you want to sit down?

MARTA: No, you sit down if you want to...

EDUARD: (*Sits*) I spend the whole day standing up... and you?

MARTA: No, I'm almost always sitting down. (*She looks out the window.*) You can see the sea from all sides...

EDUARD: Yes...

MARTA: The other time I came it was bluer than today...

Pause.

EDUARD: I tell my pupils, "Above all look... observe things..." but they never listen.... Anyway it seems to me there is hope.

MARTA: Hope?

EDUARD: Doesn't it seem so to you?

MARTA: I don't know...

EDUARD: Do you have children?

MARTA: No.

EDUARD: Then it's more difficult to have hope.... (*Pause.*) Everyone says that I take things too seriously, but deep down it's not true.

MARTA: Do you have children?

EDUARD: No, but I'd like to. It's almost the same thing.

MARTA: You think so?

EDUARD: No... well, I suppose not.... Do you believe that the flat is hers?

MARTA: Glòria's? Yes, I do.

EDUARD: You don't know for sure...

MARTA: Yes, it's hers, for sure.

Pause.

EDUARD: Are you alright?

MARTA: Yes... why...

EDUARD: I don't know...

MARTA: The truth is things haven't been good lately, but I'm fine...

EDUARD: Are you depressed?

MARTA: No, it's not quite that...

EDUARD: What is it then?

MARTA: I don't know... it's everything.

EDUARD: Aren't you happy?

MARTA: What?

EDUARD: I said, aren't you're happy?

MARTA: I don't know... well, not really, I suppose...

EDUARD gets up.

EDUARD: Now it's your turn to sit down.

MARTA: No... it's alright...

EDUARD: Come... yes... sit...

MARTA: No... you sit... really...

EDUARD: Come on... .sit. Come...

MARTA approaches the box. EDUARD makes her sit down and begin to massage her shoulders.

EDUARD: Sometimes it's all a matter of relaxation.

Pause.

MARTA: Are you happy?

EDUARD: Tell me if I press too hard...

MARTA: No, it's fine.

Pause.

EDUARD: Do you have insomnia?

MARTA: No...

EDUARD: How many hours do you sleep?

MARTA: At night? Six or seven...

EDUARD: I sleep four.

MARTA: It's very little, isn't it?

EDUARD: I can't sleep any more than that. But it's fine because this way I have more time to do other things.

MARTA: And you're not tired?

EDUARD: No... I listen to music, and I also read a lot... and sometimes I go out walking... to see the trucks taking away the rubbish.

Pause.

MARTA: What are you a master of?

EDUARD: Of mathematics, natural sciences, literature... a little of everything, except music and physical education. The PE masters are the only ones permitted to touch the pupils... when I say touch I mean put a hand on their head, or take them by the arm... of course the pupils are not allowed to touch the masters either... only pupils can touch pupils and masters touch masters. It's not like there's any written law but in fact that's how it is. (*Pause.*) They say happiness is first of all a thing of the body and then of the spirit, and not the reverse... it's not a very original theory, I know... and I don't know if it's true either...

MARTA: Listen... I'm OK now, thanks...

MARTA gets up and approaches the door. Pause.

EDUARD: Is she coming?

MARTA: No, not yet.

Pause.

EDUARD: Do you want to think of something for us to say to Glòria before she comes back? That we've been mulling over the flat...

124

MARTA: Yes, fine.

EDUARD: What will we say... let's see...

MARTA: It's better if we don't say the same thing, isn't it?

EDUARD: Yes, of course.

MARTA: Because you don't want to buy the whole flat...

EDUARD: No, I can't.

MARTA: Me neither.

EDUARD: That's clear, then.

MARTA: And renting it?

EDUARD: Renting it?

MARTA: Yes...

EDUARD: Can you rent it?

MARTA: No... but it would be better for me to rent it, the whole place... it's another thing if we share it...

EDUARD: I don't understand...

MARTA: No, look... leave it...

EDUARD: No... wait... what do you mean...

MARTA: It's OK... really...

EDUARD: Listen... if you want the whole flat, tell me...

MARTA: No... I'd sooner rent it... no, look... in fact I want to rent the flat above which is the same as this, I shouldn't have told you because Glòria told me not to tell anyone.

EDUARD: Then you came to rent the flat above.

MARTA: No, I came to find out if it's possible to rent it... Glòria came to let me know today...

EDUARD: You can't rent it.

MARTA: How do you know...

EDUARD: She told me.

MARTA: Really?

EDUARD: She told me that downstairs there were offices and upstairs was occupied and it couldn't be rented. She told me a moment ago...

MARTA: Oh...

EDUARD: I didn't ask her... she told me.... You don't believe it?

MARTA: Yes, of course... if she told you...

Pause.

EDUARD: Look... it seems to me that long-term you'd be better off buying half than renting the whole place... but it's better if we talk afterwards.... Now we have to act as if we haven't talked of anything.... Listen... if you want more time to mull it over we can also meet tomorrow... instead of today. (*Pause.*) It will be another matter if the flat doesn't really belong to Glòria...

MARTA: The one above belongs to her parents.

EDUARD: To her parents? She didn't tell me that...

MARTA: Yes, but they're never there... and because of that she told me maybe I could rent it...

EDUARD: Look... if the flat isn't hers sooner or later we'll find out.

Pause.

MARTA: Did Glòria tell you she was going to Geneva?

EDUARD: No...

MARTA: And that she would be working for the United Nations?

EDUARD: No, not that either... but we haven't talked much... suddenly she went out...

MARTA: I think she could have told me over the phone that the flat can't be rented when she called me...

EDUARD: She won't have told you because she probably couldn't find anyone else who was interested, apart from me of course.... She wants to go too quickly, I told you that before... for that reason from the start I've made out that I'm interested in the whole flat... you should've done the same, shouldn't you? Listen... if you don't want to buy half the flat I can look into arranging it some other way... of course I don't have too much time now...

MARTA: How would you arrange it?

EDUARD: What?

MARTA: The flat...

EDUARD: I don't know... I'd have to find someone else... I can tell Glòria that I'm interested in buying the whole flat... and find someone who wants half from somewhere else... of course, where will I find someone who wants half a flat now? Do you know anybody? I don't know... I'll manage I suppose... because you are definitely not interested. Look... I think that you need to think it over... if you want we can call each other a couple of days from now... it won't cost you anything... and if you tell me no then no...

MARTA: What's your phone number? (*She searches in her bag.*)

EDUARD: I can call you, if you like...

MARTA takes a card from her bag and gives it to EDUARD.

MARTA: It's old but the number is the same...

EDUARD: Is it a work number?

MARTA: Yes... it's more difficult to get me at home, I'm hardly ever there. Well... I think I'll go...

EDUARD: Now?

MARTA: Yes.

EDUARD: It will seem a bit strange to Glòria that you left without saying anything to her...

MARTA: Tell her I had to leave... that it was late...

EDUARD: Why don't you stay until she comes back? I shouldn't have told you that the flat can't be rented...

MARTA: Did she tell you not to tell me?

EDUARD: No... she didn't tell me anything... but it will seem strange to her if you don't wait... yes... wait... and when she comes back we'll tell her we've been thinking it over... that it's very expensive, the flat.... (*He looks out the window. Pause.*) Now it's... now it's not like before... the sea... like a moment ago.... I'm thinking that we could both go and when she comes back she'll find no one here, can you imagine? We could leave her a note stuck to the door saying we were in a rush... and we couldn't wait any longer... and we'll call to tell her either way. What do you think?

MARTA: I don't know...

EDUARD: Yes, come on... we'll do it... come on. (*He takes a pen from his pocket.*) Making us wait so long... do you have a piece of paper?

MARTA: You really mean it?

EDUARD: Yes, absolutely. (*He approaches the door.*) We'll hang it here... on the doorknob... OK... who will write it?

MARTA: (*Searching her bag*) Wait... I can't find any paper...

EDUARD: Or else we can hide behind the door and when she comes in give her a good shock. Have you ever done that? I don't know if we'll both fit. (*He puts himself behind the door.*) No... we won't fit...

MARTA looks at her bag.

MARTA: I have no paper to write on. (*Pause.*)Listen...

EDUARD: (*Behind the door*) Can you see me?

MARTA: What...

EDUARD: Can you see me?

MARTA: From here no.... I don't think Glòria will find all this funny.... (*Pause.*) Listen... hey, Eduard? Listen... look... I can't buy half the flat... it's better if you find someone else... I'm telling you now because this way you won't lose two days.... Glòria doesn't leave for another month... well, three weeks... she told me herself. (*Pause.*) The truth is I would've liked to rent this flat because it's very close to work... it's fairly big... and what's more, you can see the sea.... Where I live now isn't even half of this... of course I don't pay much rent...

Pause.

EDUARD: (*Still behind the door*) Have you ever loved someone?

MARTA: Yes, of course...

EDUARD: I mean really... not like everyone says they love someone... I mean in that way that only happens once, if ever.

MARTA: Do you love someone like that?

EDUARD: Yes, but I've ruined it all, absolutely.

Pause.

MARTA: What happened?

EDUARD: I ruined it forever.

MARTA: Maybe it can still be sorted out...

EDUARD: What...

MARTA: I said maybe it can still be sorted out...

EDUARD: No, now it can't be sorted out. (*Pause.*) Listen... if you want you can go... I'll tell Glòria that you've had to go.

MARTA: I... you know how I know I love someone? I mean really.... Because when he's not there all I want is for him to be with me, and when we're together that he'll never leave. (*Pause.*) Maybe that's not very well said... I don't know how to explain it...

EDUARD: No... it's fine...

MARTA: No, it's terrible...

EDUARD: No, it's a way of saying it...

MARTA: No... if I had recorded it I'd already be erasing it...

EDUARD: (*He sticks his head out from behind the door*) What?

MARTA: No... nothing.

EDUARD: How long have you been looking for a flat?

MARTA: I don't know...

EDUARD: I've been looking for six months.

MARTA: No, I've been looking longer.

EDUARD: A year?

MARTA: Yes... a little longer... but I haven't spent all the time looking... from time to time I look at the papers, and if there is something that interests me I go see it.

EDUARD: I have to find a flat soon because I sold mine to a friend that needs to set up a photography studio there soon... he's waiting for me to leave so he can go in...

Pause.

MARTA: Listen... have you ever been interviewed?

EDUARD: What?

MARTA: Have you ever been interviewed on the radio?

EDUARD: Why?

MARTA: No... it's just that now I'm in charge of an interviews programme... we interview people that, well... people who are not well-known but do something special... well, that in some way have things to say...

EDUARD: You want to interview me?

MARTA: Well, not me... I'd bring you to the studio... we'd only have to talk about you, about your work... whenever it suits you, of course... you only have to call the number on the card... and we can arrange it for another day... I'm the producer of the programme...

EDUARD: And why me?

MARTA: Well... it seems to me it could be interesting... I have a good eye for people...

EDUARD: Don't think that on the radio I'd say any of the things I've said to you...

MARTA: No... OK... Anyway, we put the questions to you.... How does it sound to you?

Pause.

EDUARD: Could I bring someone to the studio?

MARTA: Who?

EDUARD: Some pupils...

MARTA: Yes, of course, they can see how we interview you.

EDUARD: I was thinking a type of debate...

MARTA: A debate?

EDUARD: Yes... between everyone...

MARTA: This programme is only interviews... we interview one person each time... only one... there's an interviewer who asks the questions and a guest, no one else. (*Pause.*) Anyway, think it over and if you want to do it, call me.... I haven't upset you, have I?

EDUARD: Why...

MARTA: I don't know... because of everything... because I can't buy half the flat...

EDUARD: I'll find someone.

MARTA: Yes, I'm sure you will.... (*Pause.*) Well... tell Glòria I'll call her... or if not, tell her to call me.

EDUARD: Yes, I'll tell her.

MARTA: Well... goodbye...

EDUARD: Goodbye...

MARTA approaches EDUARD, gives him a kiss then goes out of the room.

EDUARD: (*Louder*) If you meet Glòria in the street tell her I don't think I'll wait here much longer...

Pause.

Blackout.

ACT THREE

The same empty room. EDUARD and GLÒRIA are reading some papers. They sign them on top of the wooden box.

EDUARD: Here as well?

GLÒRIA: Yes.

Pause. GLÒRIA takes a paper from EDUARD.

GLÒRIA: This is for me....

GLÒRIA gives EDUARD one of her papers.
They finish reading them. Pause.

EDUARD: (*Taking a cheque from his pocket.*) Here... you can cash it Monday. There was no problem with the other one, was there?

GLÒRIA: No, I cashed it immediately.

Pause.

EDUARD: It's gone well, hasn't it?

GLÒRIA: What?

EDUARD: I meant that I thought the whole thing would take longer...

GLÒRIA: Yes, well... I hope we haven't forgotten anything...

EDUARD: Do you think that we've forgotten something?

GLÒRIA: No... no... but you always think...

EDUARD: Do you want us to look over them again?

GLÒRIA: No... there's no need, we haven't forgotten anything.... Wait.... (*She searches for something.*)

EDUARD: What's wrong? (*Pause.*) I have the keys.... (*He takes them out.*)

GLÒRIA: You're missing the mailbox key. (*She looks on the ground.*)

EDUARD: Did you drop it?

GLÒRIA: I don't know... I had it a moment ago...

Both look on the ground all over the room.

EDUARD: (*While searching*) No... really now... everything has gone very well... I thought that there would be more obstacles... I don't know.... What's more, we understood each other immediately.... Of course from the beginning you were very clear...

GLÒRIA: Well... I think that you were too...

EDUARD: Yes, we were both very clear, so we understood each other.

GLÒRIA: (*Suddenly she finds the key in a pocket.*) It's here... I had it in my pocket... since it's so small.... (*She gives it to EDUARD.*)

Pause.

EDUARD: When do you go?

GLÒRIA: A week from today...

EDUARD: So soon?

GLÒRIA: Yes... I'm counting the days...

EDUARD: How would you feel about going out for dinner before you go? It seems only fair.

GLÒRIA: Yes, it does... if you want we could maybe meet some day that suits us both... I don't know...

EDUARD: Look, if it doesn't suit you it's alright...

GLÒRIA: No... let's meet...

EDUARD: We could also go out to dinner when you come back for the holidays... couldn't we?

GLÒRIA: Yes, maybe that's better...

EDUARD: I'm also very busy now with the exams.... (*Looking out the window.*) The sea... don't you think it's wonderful.... Now that I think about it, there's no sea in Switzerland...

GLÒRIA: No, there isn't...

EDUARD: I'd miss it a lot, I don't know...

Pause.

GLÒRIA: I don't know if I told you, but my parents live upstairs.... No, I didn't tell you, did I?

EDUARD: Marta told me... but I remember now she told me not to tell you.

GLÒRIA: It's alright...

EDUARD: I don't know how she knew that...

GLÒRIA: I told her. Anyway, they're never there.... They only come here from time to time.

EDUARD: I've been lucky... I've been looking for a flat like this for a long time...

GLÒRIA: How long?

EDUARD: How long? Well, I don't know, a year.... You are definitely going, aren't you?

GLÒRIA: What?

EDUARD: To Switzerland... it's absolutely definite...

GLÒRIA: Yes... of course....

EDUARD: I'm sorry... I meant that it's... you can't come back whenever you want... if you were closer it would be another thing altogether I suppose... why am I saying such awful things...

GLÒRIA: Don't think that, I'm sad to be going there... to be leaving the flat...

EDUARD: Yes, of course...

GLÒRIA: I've lived here for many years...

EDUARD: Yes, I know what you mean... Listen... why don't we at least go for a drink now? Seeing as we can't go for dinner together... and that way I can explain the plans I have for the flat to you... from now on it will be like starting again... don't you think there is hope? It seems so to me... I really mean it.... (*Looking out the window.*) The sea... every time you look at it it's different... it's incredible...

Pause.

GLÒRIA: You'll have to redecorate certainly...

EDUARD: What?

GLÒRIA: Just that you'll have to redecorate...

EDUARD: Yes, of course, but there will have to be work done before that.

GLÒRIA: What work?

EDUARD: (*Placing himself in the middle of the room*) I want to raise a wall here.

Pause.

GLÒRIA: You're making two rooms?

EDUARD: And another kitchen...

GLÒRIA: Two kitchens...

EDUARD: The two bathrooms will also have to be fixed up a bit...

GLÒRIA: It will be two flats then...

EDUARD: I'll keep one and sell the other.

GLÒRIA: To Marta?

EDUARD: To Marta? No... she didn't want to buy it.... Did she call you?

GLÒRIA: Marta? No...

EDUARD: She told me she would call you.... Here I'll make a door that will open into the room next door... what do you think?

GLÒRIA: On this side there won't be any window...

EDUARD: Yes... it's true... but it could be done... another window can be put in here...

Pause.

GLÒRIA: You'll have to get permission.

EDUARD: Permission?

GLÒRIA: From the council.

EDUARD: To make a window?

GLÒRIA: Yes, I think you have to get permission.

EDUARD: In that case perhaps I won't do it.... I'll keep this side... but don't think I'm doing it because of the window... I'm doing it for the kitchen. I'll make a new kitchen, that way the other side will be finished first. You'll see when it's done... by the holidays it will definitely all be done... yes... definitely...

GLÒRIA: Listen... what if you didn't do it up?

EDUARD: What...

GLÒRIA: The flat...

EDUARD: What do you mean...

GLÒRIA: Look... if I were you I wouldn't do any work... I would leave it as it is now, exactly the same...

EDUARD: Why?

GLÒRIA: Have you had someone really look at the flat?

EDUARD: Really?

GLÒRIA: Yes...

Pause.

EDUARD: Listen... what's the matter...

GLÒRIA: It's been a while since the offices downstairs have been rented by anybody.

EDUARD: And what... what do you mean by that...

141

GLÒRIA: Already my parents don't dare to come... it seems to me that they are scared it will collapse one day on top of their only daughter, can you imagine? No... I'm exaggerating now...

EDUARD: Do you mean the building is derelict?

GLÒRIA: No, derelict, no.... Listen...

EDUARD: And why has nothing been put up outside?

GLÒRIA: Outside?

EDUARD: I meant when a building is derelict... they pull it down... or they put a warning up outside... yes, they close it so no one goes near it... that's what they do... isn't it?

GLÒRIA: You mean the council?

EDUARD: Yes, the council or whoever...

GLÒRIA: No one knows, only my parents and I.

EDUARD: And why are you telling me now?

GLÒRIA: The truth is I wasn't going to tell you at all, but if you want to do work it's different... look, I think that if the building isn't touched, then it will last for some years yet.

EDUARD: I can't believe it...

GLÒRIA: If you don't build the wall in the middle... if you only make a new kitchen maybe there won't be any danger...

EDUARD: Listen...

GLÒRIA: Look... I've been here a long time and I've never had a problem... otherwise I wouldn't have sold you the flat... if I'd known all this I wouldn't have sold you the flat...

EDUARD: Listen... give me back the cheque...

GLÒRIA: What...

EDUARD: The cheque I just gave you... come on... or if not it doesn't matter... I'll call the bank... there's no telephone here, it's true...

GLÒRIA: I wasn't going to cash it...

EDUARD: And the other?

GLÒRIA: What...

EDUARD: The other cheque!

GLÒRIA: What's the matter?

EDUARD: Have you cashed it?

GLÒRIA: Yes, I already told you I had.

EDUARD: Then you have to give me back the money. Do you understand me?

Pause.

GLÒRIA: I can't give it back to you.

EDUARD: You sold me a derelict flat, didn't you? So give me back the money right now...

GLÒRIA: I sold you half... you have a whole flat at half the price.

EDUARD: What...

GLÒRIA: In fact now it's as if you had sold the half... isn't it?

EDUARD: Incredible...

GLÒRIA: If you'd told me right at the beginning that you were thinking of dividing the flat I wouldn't have sold it to you.

EDUARD: I don't believe this...

GLÒRIA: You didn't tell me, did you?

EDUARD: Will you give me back the money or not?

GLÒRIA: I didn't have to say anything, like you didn't... I could have gone to Geneva without telling you anything.

EDUARD: Of course... and then it collapses on top of me, right?

GLÒRIA: That's why I told you, only because of that.

EDUARD: Like I should thank you... incredible...

GLÒRIA: Anyone else in my place wouldn't have told you... they'd have gone without saying a word.

EDUARD: Listen, you don't want a messy situation do you? You don't want me to mess you up? Then give me back the money right now...

GLÒRIA: It's not possible.

EDUARD: Why isn't it possible?

GLÒRIA: Because I've spent it.

EDUARD: You've spent all the money?

GLÒRIA: Almost all of it.

Pause.

EDUARD: So... what will we do now... tell me what we'll do... eh!

GLÒRIA: I don't know.

EDUARD: I'll demand it from your parents.

GLÒRIA: From my parents?

EDUARD: I'm sure they won't want their daughter in a real mess... because now you're in a real mess, I don't know if you know that...

GLÒRIA: They're not there...

EDUARD: What...

GLÒRIA: They're not there now, my parents...

EDUARD: Oh no?

GLÒRIA: No, I told you before, they're not there...

EDUARD: And why should I believe you, eh?

GLÒRIA: Listen...

EDUARD: Well... come on... we'll go up.... (*Pause.*) Are you coming or not!

GLÒRIA: There's no need for us to go up...

EDUARD: So I'll make them come down... it's all the same... you'll see they'll come down in a hurry...

GLÒRIA: Wait... it's not true...

EDUARD: What...

GLÒRIA: The flat thing... it's not true. It was a joke.

EDUARD: A joke?

GLÒRIA: Yes, I played a joke on you... I thought you wouldn't believe it...

EDUARD: But...

GLÒRIA: I thought you'd realise straight away that it was a joke...

Pause.

146

EDUARD: So you've been pulling my leg all the time... is that what you mean?

GLÒRIA: It was only a joke.... You don't believe it? Listen... if you want call whoever... the council if you want...

EDUARD: The council?

GLÒRIA: Because they'll look at the building, if you call them right now...

Pause.

EDUARD: Why did you wait so long to tell me?

GLÒRIA: I don't know... because it was a joke... I thought you wouldn't believe it...

Pause.

EDUARD: Then I've been taken in. (*He laughs.*)

GLÒRIA: I thought you'd realise straight away... the truth is I don't know why I did it...

EDUARD: I was going to see your parents... like at school... how ridiculous.... Well, in fact I wouldn't have done that even in school.

GLÒRIA: At least you didn't say you were going to the police...

EDUARD: No... I was thinking of doing that afterwards... if you hadn't found your parents... it's mad, isn't it?

GLÒRIA: No, not if you believed it...

EDUARD: That's it precisely... I believed it...

GLÒRIA: I'm sorry...

EDUARD: No, it's my fault...

GLÒRIA: Well... I don't know what I would have done, in your place...

EDUARD: You wouldn't have believed it, I'm sure.

GLÒRIA: Maybe I would have, I don't know...

EDUARD: No, you did it very well, really... I swallowed it all...

Pause.

GLÒRIA: There was a moment that I was going to say... that it was all a joke...

EDUARD: Oh yes... when?

GLÒRIA: Almost at the start... when you asked me if the building was derelict... but I didn't.... Now don't think I do this often... actually, it's the first time...

EDUARD: And if I hadn't said I was going to see your parents we'd still be here, wouldn't we?

GLÒRIA: No... no, I was going to tell you... in the end I would have told you...

148

EDUARD: Did you do this to Marta as well? A joke like this...

GLÒRIA: No... I didn't do it to anyone else...

EDUARD: Of course, you could only do it to whoever took the flat...

GLÒRIA: But I didn't have it thought out... you think I had it thought out... I didn't even know you were going to make two flats...

EDUARD: No, of course.... Are your parents really upstairs or not...

GLÒRIA: No, they're not there. They only come here from time to time... every time it's harder for them to move from one place to the other, they're old... and as the lift only comes up... I told you that before, didn't I? And that one has to be careful to close the door each time? Yes, I told you that too.... If any letter arrives for me you can leave it in my parents' postbox, and they'll send it to me.

EDUARD: If you want I can send them to you myself...

GLÒRIA: There's no need...

EDUARD: Your parents only come from time to time, don't they?

GLÒRIA: Yes...

EDUARD: If I send them to you, you'll certainly get them much sooner...

GLÒRIA: Yes, but I feel bad...

EDUARD: It makes no difference to me.

GLÒRIA: Anyway I don't think much will come, most likely some bill... (*She lifts up the wooden box and takes out the door handle from underneath.*) It's from one of the bathrooms/ toilets, it fell off the other day and I left it here... I don't think it can be fixed...

EDUARD takes the handle from GLÒRIA.

GLÒRIA: If the box bothers you you can throw it away as well.

EDUARD: I never throw anything away... everything can be used for something else... and if I can't use it, I give it to someone else.... There should be a subject at school that deals with fixing things. Just that, "fixing things".

Pause.

GLÒRIA: Listen... can I ask you a favour?

EDUARD: Yes, of course...

GLÒRIA: Before I go away will you let me spend some time alone here... in the flat? It's something I should have done before... but as everything happened so fast I didn't have any time...

EDUARD: Yes, of course, whenever you want... whenever it suits you...

GLÒRIA: I can come tomorrow or the day after... but if it doesn't suit you, tell me...

EDUARD: Whenever you want...

GLÒRIA: I can call you beforehand...

EDUARD: Listen... if you want you could stay now...

GLÒRIA: Now?

EDUARD: If it suits you, of course...

GLÒRIA: You don't mind?

EDUARD: No... and this way you don't have to come another day...

GLÒRIA: Yes... well...

Pause.

EDUARD: So you're staying?

GLÒRIA: Yes... thank you...

EDUARD: Well... I'm going. We'll speak before you go away...

GLÒRIA: Yes...

EDUARD goes out of the room. After a few moments he returns.

EDUARD: Excuse me... but I was thinking what should we do with the key... I mean should you keep it or should I take it... because you don't have a copy, do you?

GLÒRIA: No...

EDUARD: Look... if I only close the door without locking it, fully... the flat is empty, even if someone comes in...

GLÒRIA: Wait... there's no need, I'll leave with you...

EDUARD: You're not staying?

GLÒRIA: No, I'll come another day.

Pause.

EDUARD: Do you want me to stay in another room?

GLÒRIA: What?

EDUARD: While you're here... I won't make a sound... it will be like there's no one else here.

GLÒRIA: No, it doesn't matter...

EDUARD: I can also stay on this side of the room... as if there were the wall in the middle... wait... (*He goes behind the door.*) Can you see me?

GLÒRIA: No...

EDUARD: (*Behind the door*) Now I won't say another word... really...

Pause.

GLÒRIA: Listen... there's no need...

EDUARD: (*Poking his head out from behind the door.*) What? (*He emerges from behind the door.*)

GLÒRIA: Look... if you want you can go... there's no need for you to stay.

EDUARD: Are you staying?

GLÒRIA: Yes.

Pause.

EDUARD: So I'll take the keys?

GLÒRIA: Yes, you keep them.

EDUARD: Well... goodbye then...

GLÒRIA: Goodbye.

EDUARD gives GLÒRIA a kiss and leaves the room. Pause. GLÒRIA walks to the window.

GLÒRIA: Listen...

Pause.

Blackout.

Biographies

Joan Casas

Joan Casas has written plays, fiction, poetry and essays as well as working extensively as a translator into Catalan and Spanish; with Nina Avrova he has translated Chekhov's complete dramatic works into Catalan. His play *Nus* (*Naked*) won the Ignasi Iglésias Prize (1990) and *Corporal Nocturne* (*Nocturn Corporal*) was awarded the Ciutat d'Alcoi Prize for Theatre (1993). More recent works include *El Vincle* and *Elles mateixes*. His plays have been translated into Russian and Spanish. Joan currently teaches Dramaturgy and Theatre Criticism.

Jordi Coca

Jordi Coca was born in Barcelona in 1947. He has become a leading figure in Catalan culture and literature, working in the fields of narrative fiction, drama, poetry, criticism and translation. He has published over thirty works and has won numerous literary prizes, from the Serra d'Or for young writers (1972) to the Premi Carlemany (2007). *Under the Dust* (*Sota la Pols*) won the prestigious Premi Sant Jordi in 2000. He has been actively involved in Catalan politics over many years and is a regular contributor to Catalan newspapers and television. He lives in Barcelona.

Lluïsa Cunillé

Lluïsa Cunillé studied textual dramaturgy with José Sanchis Sinisterra at the Sala Beckett, Barcelona, before co-founding, in 1995, the Companyia Hongaresa de Teatre (Hungarian Theatre Company). Her play *Roundabout* received the Calderón de la Barca Prize (1991). *Accident* won the Institute of Catalan Letters Prize (1997) and

Barcelona, Map of Shadows was awarded the City of Barcalona Prize for Theatre (2004). She writes in Catalan and Spanish and her work has been translated into French, Italian and English. As well as plays she writes 'some of the best works of cabaret in Catalan theatre' (Institut Ramon Llull).

Jeff Teare

Jeff Teare has directed over one hundred theatre productions, ranging from puppet shows for the under-fives to Chekhov, Pinter, Shakespeare, etc. He has also written numerous performed plays, has made various videos/documentaries and edited several books. He is currently an Honorary Fellow of the University of Plymouth.

Peter Bush

Peter Bush works in Barcelona as a freelance literary translator. He was awarded the Valle-Inclán Literary Translation Prize for his translation of Juan Goytisolo's *The Marx Family Saga*. He edited (with Susan Bassnett) *The Translator as Writer* and put together the anthology of Cuban stories *The Voice of the Turtle*. Recent translations include *I Love You When I'm Drunk* by Empar Moliner, *Havana Gold* by Leonardo Padura and *The Enormity of the Tragedy* by Quim Monzó. Current projects include Goytisolo's *Juan the Landless* and *A Not So Perfect Crime* by Teresa Solana.

Laura McGloughlin

Laura McGloughlin has been working as a freelance translator from Spanish and Catalan since completing a Masters in Literary Translation at the University of East Anglia in 2006. She lives in London.

Richard Thomson

Richard Thomson moved to Catalonia in 1986. His translation of Jordi Coca's *Under the Dust* was published in 2007 and *Look Me in the Eye* by Sílvia Soler in 2008. His translations of Francesc Serés and Pere Guixà's short stories are included in *New Catalan Fiction* (Dalkey Archive Press' Review of Contemporary Fiction, 2008). He now lives on a farm in Wales.